ONE GIRL CAN MAKE A DIFFERENCE

© 2023 MARVEL

All rights reserved. Published by Marvel Press, an imprint of Buena Vista Books, Inc.
No part of this book may be reproduced or transmitted in any form or by any means,
electronic or mechanical, including photocopying, recording, or by any information storage
and retrieval system, without written permission from the publisher.
For information address Marvel Press, 77 West 66th Street, New York, New York 10023.

Printed in the United States of America
First Paperback Edition, August 2023
10 9 8 7 6 5 4 3 2 1
FAC-025438-23159
Library of Congress Control Number: 2021945906
ISBN 978-1-368-07737-8

Visit www.disneybooks.com and www.marvel.com.
Visit www.disneychannel.com.

SUSTAINABLE
FORESTRY
INITIATIVE

Certified Sourcing

www.sfiprogram.org
SFI-01054

The SFI label applies to the text stock

ONE GIRL CAN
MAKE A DIFFERENCE

By Michelle Meadows

Based on the episode written by
Jeffrey M. Howard
and **Kate Kondell**

Illustrations by
Gianfranco Florio and **Manny Mederos**

Designed by
Megan R. Youngquist

MARVEL

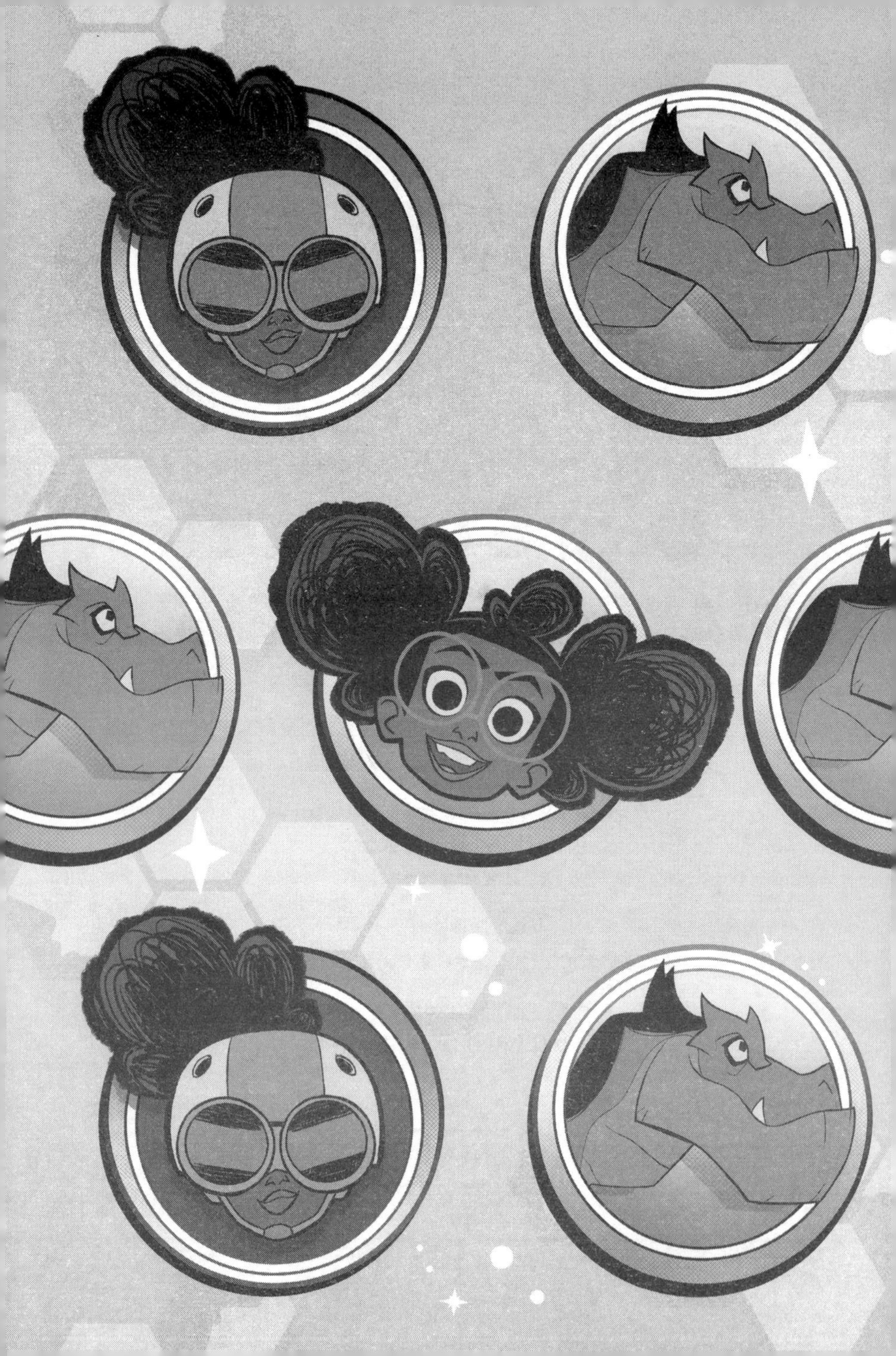

CHAPTER ONE

My name is Lunella Lafayette, and if you told me two months ago that I would make a real friend at school, get my own dinosaur, and become a Super Hero, I never would have believed you. Not in a zillion years. Here's how it all went down:

It started on a Saturday morning when I was roller-skating through New York City's Lower East Side, also known as the LES— also known as *the* best neighborhood on the planet. There's a rhythm to our streets that I can always count on. And I'm not just talking about the music of my skate wheels gliding across the pavement.

That day, there was the *whoosh-whoosh* of water blasting out of a fire hydrant. Kids played and laughed, and a cool mist sprayed my legs as I jumped over an arc of water. Rappers dropped rhymes on a street corner, and I danced down a whole block. There was the *clink-clank* of shop owners setting up and getting ready for a new day.

"Here comes Lunella!" Mr. Septimus yelled as he leaned out of his pawn shop and flipped his sign to OPEN.

"Hola, Lunella!" Señora Martinez said as she swept her bodega's sidewalk.

"Hola, Señora. Buenos días," I called out.

But hold up—wait a minute. I skidded to a stop when I saw the OUT OF BUSINESS sign hanging on the door of Bubbe Bina's Knish Niche. Bubbe Bina is a sweet old lady with silver curls who knows that my favorite knish is round and stuffed with mashed potatoes, cheese, and her top secret sauce. One morning Bubbe Bina's credit card machine had malfunctioned, and I could tell she was stressed out. I was late for school, but I fixed her machine as fast as I could. Bubbe Bina said I saved her life, and she gave me free knishes for a month!

I skated up close to the window and looked inside the store. All the tables and chairs were gone. The case where the knishes were usually displayed was totally empty.

Ahmed stepped out from his store next door, Ahmed's Deli. He handed me my favorite breakfast sandwich, and I thanked him with a fist bump. Ahmed always hooks me up.

"What happened to Bubbe Bina's place?" I asked, peeling back the sandwich wrapper.

"It's those blackouts we've been havin,'" Ahmed said. "Lost batches mean lost business. So they put the kibosh on the knish."

"Aw, that's horrible," I said. "Those knishes were knish-a-licious!"

While I ate, we both kept staring through the window as if Bubbe Bina's Knish Niche might magically reappear. Still empty. I had overheard my parents talking at home about how random blackouts were causing trouble, shutting down power throughout the neighborhood. But I never thought it could put anyone out of business. I thought about how my dad had told me knishes have a long history in the LES. Jewish immigrants brought knishes to America more than one hundred years ago, and we got knishes in our neighborhood first.

"At least your family's spot is hoppin'," Ahmed said. He looked across the street at Roll With It, my family's roller-skating rink. The thing about the mom-and-pop shops in the LES is that I grew up with the shop owners on our street. I talk with them way more than I talk with any of the kids at school. And it's a big deal when a shop owner has to put up an OUT OF BUSINESS sign and clear everything out, because it's like all their hopes and dreams got cleared out, too. I wondered if Bubbe Bina would be okay without her shop.

I skated over to Roll With It to check things out. Our rink is easy to spot because it's shaped different from all the buildings around it. Our place has a round dome on top and a glowing neon sign shaped like an arrow pointing right up to the sky. My grandpa, Pops, always wanted to own his own roller rink because when he was growing up roller rinks were segregated. Pops decided he wanted to build a rink where everybody could skate.

When I rolled inside, the rink was packed and music was thumping. Roll With It is known as the heartbeat of the LES. For one thing, the rink has been around a long time, while other businesses have come and gone. And for another, the rink brings all kinds of people together to have fun.

The last blackout had messed up some of

our equipment, so I made adjustments on a circuit board to fix my mom's sound mixer.

"Mixer's good to go, Mom!" I shouted when I was done. She blew me a kiss from her DJ booth. Mom is in charge of keeping the music flowing, and she also uses her microphone to share her pearls of wisdom.

I rolled over to help my grandma Mimi. She runs our snack bar, Mimi's Morsels. She needed me to fix a coil on her fryer.

"Thank you, sweet child," said Mimi. She gave me a hug and told the customers, "We're back, y'all! And these wings are as spicy as the lady who made 'em."

Pops was dancing on the skate floor. My grandpa is a really cool dude. I love dancing with him because nobody has his moves. He taught me everything I know about roller-skating, especially how to turn, stop, dance, and jump without falling on my face.

Pops motioned for me to come over and dance with him.

"Coming!" I called out, and rolled toward him. "Would I say no to the longest-reigning Roller Jam King? Never! Do I look like a fool?" Me and Pops know we can jam. Soon a crowd circled us to watch. Even though Pops is my father's dad, somehow my dad didn't get the roller-skating gene . . . or the dancing gene. Pops says the rhythm department skipped right over him. But Dad makes up for it because he's the one who comes up with the creative ideas to bring customers to the rink.

Mom leaned into her mic and said, "Don't sweat those blackouts, Lower East Side! They can take our light, but they can't take our spirit!" The crowd roared. And for a while, I completely forgot about the blackouts.

And then *whoomp!* The lights cut out. The music stopped. Another blackout. Customers grumbled and groaned, "Not again! Not another blackout." We waited a few minutes, but the power didn't come back. It's hard to skate in the dark with no music. Disappointed customers started returning their skates.

"Sorry, folks," Dad said. "Here's your money back. . . . Please roll with us again. Man. Somebody has got to fix this."

I felt bad seeing my dad giving all those refunds. Especially with so many hours to go before closing time. Roll With It was done for the day.

"How many blackouts is that this month?" Mimi asked.

"Too many, baby," Pops said.

After everybody left, I asked, "Are we gonna lose the business? Like the knish shop?"

"Hey, now, we'll get through it," Dad said.

"Together our family can get through anything," Mom said.

"And what do we do when the going gets tough?" Dad said.

"We roll with it," Pops said.

"We surely do," Mimi said.

Then we all came together for our family Roll With It dance. Dad can barely do the dance, especially in the dark. He tries hard, though, and that always makes me laugh.

"That's right," Dad said. "We roll with it. What do we do, Lu?"

"We roll with it," I mumbled. But deep down, I wasn't so sure. I made a mental note to research power outages when I got home.

It's funny how when it comes to science, I love uncertainty. Every time I do a science experiment, I have a theory. I might think I know what's going to happen, but when I test it out, the outcome could be totally different. There are all kinds of variables and unknowns. That kind of uncertainty is exciting.

But when it comes to my life, there are some things I want to know 100 percent. Like that my family and my neighborhood are doing okay. And for all thirteen years of my life so far, the Lower East Side was doing okay. We were all doing okay. Until I found out we weren't.

I knew I had to fix things. I just had to figure out how.

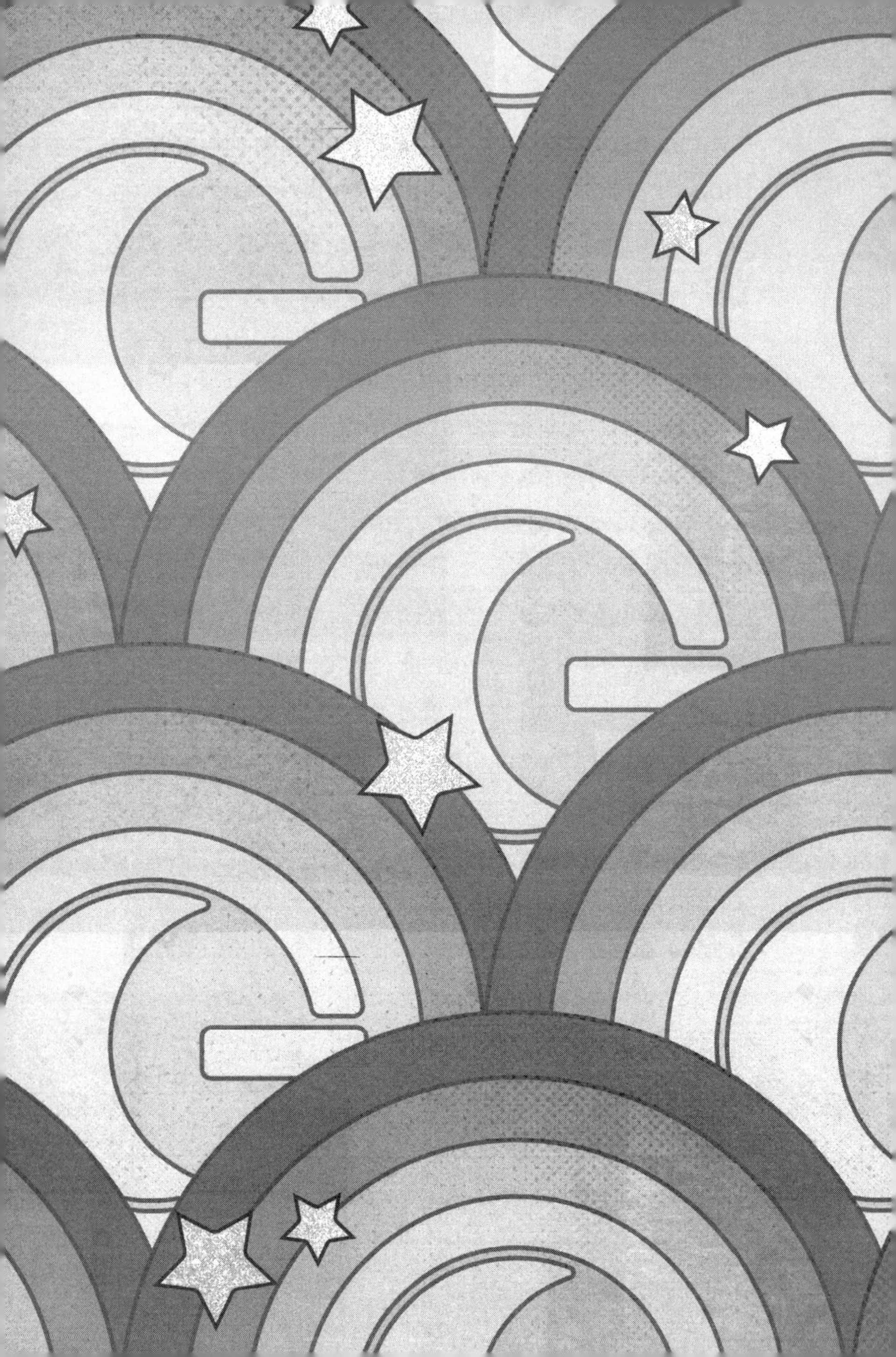

CHAPTER TWO

● ●

On Monday in the cafeteria, ketchup dripped all over my shirt while I was eating lunch. That's because I was totally in the zone. My head was in my engineering notebook as I analyzed formulas and designs. I felt like I was making progress figuring out how to help the LES get a power grid.

My mom supports my interest in research and all my projects, but she says I need to work on being more approachable. She thinks

I shouldn't bury my head in a notebook every minute of my life and that I should take time to talk to other kids more. But I never know what to say to them. I once researched some things I could ask them. Kind of like conversation starters. I even wrote them down on note cards and memorized them. Things like "What did you do over the weekend?" and "Are you trying out for the basketball team?" and "Do you think the cafeteria will have tater tots today?"

But I accidentally ended up asking some kids the same question. And let's just say they noticed. Imagine asking five people in the same week if there would be tater tots in the cafeteria. Some of them talked about me and called me weird. Even I admit that I sounded like a robot. I dumped the note cards in the trash.

Just as I was taking another bite of my french fries, one of my classmates, Eduardo, shoved a mixed-up puzzle cube in my face.

"Do the thing. Do the thing," Eduardo said, smirking and waving his friends over.

The next thing I knew, a small crowd had gathered around to watch me solve the puzzle. Even Coach Hbrek, our PE-turned-substitute-science teacher, came over to watch.

"For real, Eduardo—again?" I said. Eduardo tries to stump me with the puzzle cube all the time, but I always solve it. I was so annoyed because he was interrupting my progress on the power generator project. I miss the days when I used to sneak food into the school library and hide during lunch. I got away with it for years because the library is huge. But one day the librarian caught me, and that was the end of that.

Well, with a crowd watching, I felt pressure to solve the puzzle.

I studied the cube for a few seconds. Then I put the cube behind my back and twisted and turned it with both hands. Another student, Anand, leaned over my shoulder. He is the second-smartest kid at school, and he can't stand that I'm the smartest. So he spies on me a lot.

He once asked me how I got so smart. I didn't tell him. But the real reason is because my brain is like a super sponge. It soaks everything up, whether I want it to or not. I have to be careful about what I read and watch. Because once I see something, it seeps right into my brain forever. School can get boring because after I read the books or handouts, I know it all. When I was in third grade, I kept finishing tests and quizzes so fast that everybody called me a show-off. So I figured out a trick where I pretend like I'm still working, but I'm really all done and just daydreaming about my latest inventions.

"What's that?" Anand said, tapping on my engineering notebook. "I mean, I totally get it 'cause I'm awesome at math, but like, what is this?"

Lucky for him, I love talking about my engineering notebook.

"So glad you asked, Anand. I think it's some kind of crazy power generator, but I can't be sure. See, there was this super-cool scientist. We only know her by her code name, Moon Girl, and she was working on a top secret project for the space program, but then she just up and vanished a long time ago, and all that's left of her work are these incomplete blueprints I found on the Internet and—"

"BEEP, BEEP, BEEP! Nerd alert. Level five nerd alert," Eduardo said. I ignored him. His nerd alerts used to bother me, until I found a research study that said so-called nerds are three times more likely to become billionaires than non-nerds are. I always say the truth is in the data.

I pretended I didn't hear Eduardo and turned toward Anand.

"If I can crack this, the Lower East Side will have its own power grid: a network of electrical transmission lines that connect a bunch of generating stations to loads over a humongous area. Meaning no more black-outs. Meaning business back to usual and our neighborhood saved."

As soon as I solved the puzzle, I pulled the cube from behind my back and smiled.

"Done!" I announced, placing the puzzle cube on the table. Coach Hbrek started clapping, and then other kids in the crowd clapped, too.

"Sick!" Eduardo said.

"I can do that," Anand said. "You may have solved the puzzle, but you seem to have trouble eating without causing a ketchup explosion." I heard laughter, and I lifted my notebook and held it in front of me to hide the stains on my shirt. And just like that, my five minutes of puzzle-cube fame were over.

The crowd vanished, and Eduardo pointed to the other side of the cafeteria.

"She's filming again," Eduardo said.

He was talking about a girl named Casey Calderon. I had noticed her before, but we had never spoken. There was something about her that I liked. She asked a lot of questions and was often engrossed in a project. I heard she posted on social media all day and night. Whenever I saw her, she was either alone and on her phone or she was interviewing someone and recording videos.

Casey spoke into her camera phone:

"Hey, guys, Casey Maria Eva Duarte Goldberg-Calderon here with a big shout-out to Bertha in the cafeteria—but I have to ask: What's the deal with chicken-fried steak, anyway? Is it chicken, or is it steak? Comment below and be sure to hit that 'like' button, people."

A few seconds later, Casey shrieked.

"Eduardo, I know that was you!" Casey shouted. "You gave me a thumbs-down."

Casey whipped her head around to find Eduardo laughing.

I noticed that Casey and I were both sitting alone at lunch. We looked at each other for a second, and she smiled at me. Then she went back to looking at her phone. At the time, I had no idea that we would soon have a life-changing encounter.

CHAPTER THREE

I couldn't wait for school to end so I could get back outside with my latest invention— super-speedy wheels for roller-skating. These were the biggest wheels I had ever designed, which made me zoom around faster than ever. I made them with extra-durable material because the set of wheels I made before didn't last as long as I had hoped. As soon as the final bell rang, I ran out of the building and popped the wheels out from inside my sneakers. I rolled over to my family's rink in record time. Even from across the street, I noticed blue splotches of paint all over the rink's entrance. I knew exactly what that meant, so I sped up and rushed through the door.

"What happened?" I asked, racing over to Pops. His usual smile was gone, and he looked worn out.

"Everything's all right, sweetheart," Pops said. He grabbed my shoulder and gave it a squeeze. "Some robbers tried to come in here during a blackout. But thanks to you, nothing was taken." I had set up our rink's security system to release a forceful spray of bright blue paint, splattering anyone who tried to breach the system.

Mimi said, "That's right. Your battery-powered security system with that sweet surprise inside worked like a charm. Lord, would I like to see those thieves now."

Dad stuck his head out of his office and jumped up when he saw me.

"Lunella," Dad said. "Ahmed wasn't so lucky. He is okay, but the robbers cleaned out his deli. Even took the cold cuts." I gasped and put my hand over my mouth. Dad gave me a hug. He knew how much I loved Ahmed.

"I can't believe they took cold cuts," I said.

"Cold indeed," Pops said. "Maybe they were hungry."

Mom paced back and forth in front of the DJ booth. She seemed like she was talking to herself, but we could hear her loud and clear.

"Blackouts mean more crime," Mom said. "Some people will see them as their chance to get more of what they need. And that can lead to lost business, which means we get pushed out of the community we love! I am not raising my baby in New Jersey! No disrespect to New Jersey." Mom always says that about New Jersey because she loves living in New York City. Over the years, some of the other LES businesses that closed up shop moved to New Jersey.

"What's causing these blackouts?" I asked. "There haven't been any storms. No high winds. Has anybody been digging underground in the neighborhood or something?"

Pops looked up at me. He was tinkering with a broken roller skate. "The power company has no idea what's causing the outages," Pops said. "It's a mystery."

"I think somebody should call the Avengers!" I said. "Bet they could solve it."

Mimi said, "Sweetheart, I'm afraid the Avengers got bigger fish to fry. Besides, do they even go below Fourteenth Street?"

"We just have to roll with it, baby," Dad said.

I knew they were right. The Avengers weren't coming. But the burglary attempt was proof that I needed to fast-track my power generator plan.

Pops knew I was worried. He asked, "Did I ever tell you that when I was young, I did a quadruple axel on skates without spilling one drop of my root beer?" Pops says things like that sometimes when he wants to cheer me up, and it always works.

"Impossible," I said, laughing. "Physics says, 'Nope! Didn't happen,' Pops!"

At home in my room, I kicked off my sneakers and stretched out on my bed to think for a minute. Mom bugs me all the time to clean my room, but I'm way too busy. Plus, I know exactly where everything is. I took a deep breath and closed my eyes. Then I looked up at all my idols for inspiration. My walls are filled with posters of Spider-Man, Iron Man, and Wakanda's Shuri, plus First Lady Michelle Obama, mathematician Katherine Johnson, chemical engineer Frances Arnold, astronaut Mae Jemison, and roller derby queen Rosetta Saunders.

Dad thinks it's weird that I talk to my posters, but they are more than just posters to me. Talking with them makes me feel like I know them, and they give me the best advice. That evening, Michelle Obama told me Black girls have power. Katherine Johnson told me everything in the world is physics and math. Iron Man told me sometimes you gotta run before you walk. Just like when he took off in his prototype suit even though he wasn't exactly sure it would work.

I worked on my power generator design for about an hour before Mom tiptoed in and put a plate of snacks on my desk.

"Still working on that thing that's gonna fix all our problems?" Mom asked.

"Yep, it's like you always say. One girl can make a difference, right?"

Mom said, "Absolutely—especially when that girl is you. I may not be able to help you with whatever all this is. But I can help you with some inspiration."

Then she reached out and placed a strange device in front of me on the desk. I didn't have the heart to tell her I had no idea what it was.

"Wow . . . cool. Thanks, Mom."

"Does that say 'radioactive'?" Mom asked as she leaned over my papers and color-coded notes. "You're not actually building this thing, right?"

"Course not. Purely theoretical."

Mom breathed a sigh of relief. "Good. No radioactive stuff in the apartment. Never thought I'd hear those words come out of my mouth."

As soon as Mom left and closed my door, I locked it. My family knows if my door is locked, that means "Do Not Disturb Under Any Circumstances Ever." I grabbed my design and walked toward the closet. I'm certain I have the most interesting closet in the Lower East Side. I modified it with a super-secret pull string. All I have to do is pull it, and my whole closet turns into an elevator! I stepped inside, and the elevator car descended. When the doors opened, I pulled levers and flipped switches until bright lights flickered on and lit up my secret lab.

My lab is totally awesome! I work out of an old subway car in an abandoned subway station. It's like a lab within a lab. And just keeping it real—my power generator might be a tiny bit radioactive, but technically it's not in the apartment.

Down there is where I keep a picture of my favorite idol. I keep this image in the lab for my eyes only. It's a grainy old black-and-white photo of a bunch of white male scientists watching a young Black woman—Moon Girl—do her thing at a blackboard. Her incomplete blueprints from decades ago helped me complete my power generator project.

"What's up, Moon Girl?" I said, staring at the picture.

I put on my goggles and got to work with my finishing touches. I connected circuits, drilled pieces, and installed them.

I turned to Moon Girl. "Impressed, right? You know you impressed! But should I try it?"

My home monitor buzzed. It's connected

to the kitchen, and I use it to snoop. I know that's wrong, but sometimes I need to know what's going on. I heard my parents talking low, almost whispering.

"How are the books looking?" Mom asked.

"It's bad," Dad said. "If things don't turn around quick, we may need to sell the rink."

I knew this already because I help with the bookkeeping. Dad calls me his human calculator. I had noticed they were losing money. But to hear them say it was like a punch in the gut. The home monitor went quiet. I couldn't let my family lose the roller rink. It meant everything to our family. I wasn't sure if my power generator would work, but ready or not, I had to try.

"Here we go!" I said, firing up the device. "Let's juice this up!" Buttons lit up. The generator whirred and came to life. I watched the electrical power readings climb higher and higher.

"It's working? Yes! Yes!" I shouted. But soon I heard *BEEP, BEEP, BEEP*. A red alert flashed. The power readings climbed out of control way too fast—off the charts.

"No, no!" I knew this was really bad. "Too much juice!" I started to panic. My heart raced. I could see the device had projected a beam of energy. There was a glowing portal right in the middle of my lab! I gasped. Hold up—it hit me. This was not a power generator. I recognized that glowing light. This was a portal generator. I lunged and reached for the OFF switch on the device. But it was too late.

A gigantic creature walked right through the portal. I dropped my notebook and stepped back. I knew right away what it was. I just couldn't believe it. Humongous head. Sweaty-looking scales. Pointy teeth. Yellow glowing eyes. Black claws. It was a dinosaur. A red *Tyrannosaurus rex*. I was terrified and enthralled all at the same time. I knew he was a dinosaur, but there was something friendly about his eyes. My feet were glued to the floor. And then I remembered something I had learned at dinosaur camp. The *T. rex* had sixty teeth, to be exact. Teeth like knives that could literally crush bones.

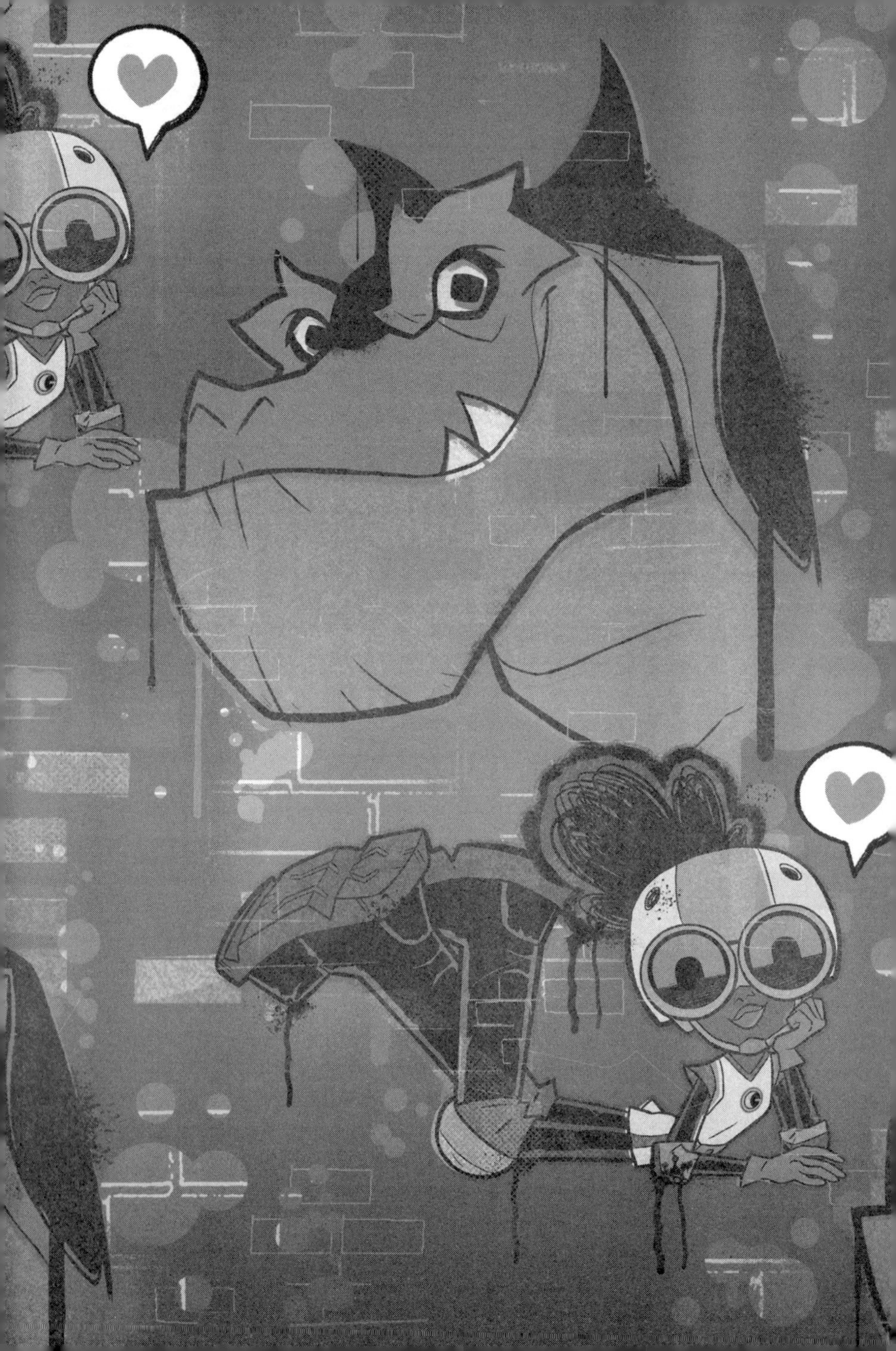

CHAPTER FOUR

Part of me wanted to crawl into a hole and hide. But a bigger part of me thought this *T. rex* was the coolest thing ever! A theropod standing right before my eyes. All the way from the Cretaceous period, millions of years ago. It was a scientist's dream come true.

"OMG!" I shouted, staring up at him. "So *cooool!*"

His beautiful red scales glistened, and his claws were incredible. He grunted, looked at me, and then sniffed up and down the tunnel walls. Even though he appeared ferocious, he didn't seem interested in eating me. That was a relief. But the reality hit me that I had just brought a dinosaur to New York City. I could hear his raspy breathing, and with every breath, my heart thumped faster and faster.

My grandma Mimi told me to think of comforting words if I ever start to panic. She said for most people, it's a poem or an inspirational saying. For me, it's the scientific method. I kept my eye on the dinosaur and began reciting the steps in my mind: ask a question, observe, form a hypothesis, experiment. . . .

Then with a flash of light and a bang, the portal closed completely. The dinosaur did something I hadn't considered as a possibility. He bolted and ran down the subway tunnel, which meant he could soon end up in the street.

"ROOOOAR!"

"Oh, snap—*wait!*" I yelled. "Not cool, not cool."

I took off after him. For a split second, I thought about popping the wheels out of my sneakers, but decided against it. I figured his moves could be unpredictable, and I needed to be able to run.

The tunnel was longer than I thought. By the time we got to the end, I was out of breath. The only thing between us and the street was a metal grate. At first, he gently tapped the grate with his snout. Then he rammed it. He plowed right through.

When we emerged from the tunnel, it was dark outside. As usual, I was wearing dark clothes, so I blended in with the night. But I knew the dinosaur wouldn't blend in. I couldn't see that well, but I spotted something shimmery. And I recognized a familiar voice.

Casey Calderon stood on the street corner filming with her phone.

"Hey, guys. Casey here, talking to people about their fav blackout attire. We may lose our light, but we will *not* lose our sparkle."

The dinosaur moved in Casey's direction, but she didn't seem to notice.

"Watch out!" I yelled.

"Whoaaa!" Casey said as the dinosaur raced past her. I was right behind him.

"Hey!" I called after him. "Come back here! Please don't eat New York City!"

It didn't take long for people to notice a humongous creature in the street. Lower East Side residents screamed. Some pointed and whipped out their phones. I heard one lady say she was calling 911. Cars crashed and horns honked. Most everybody on foot ran in the opposite direction. Except for me and Casey. I ran after the dinosaur, and Casey ran after me.

The dinosaur's tail thrashed from side to side, banging into cars. He smashed a few car windows, but nobody got hurt. He squealed and stumbled around so much that I started worrying about him. I didn't want anyone to hurt him.

I shouted, "Hey, dinosaur! No! Stop! Stop!"

Suddenly, the dinosaur stopped in his tracks.

"Well, that was easy," I said. "You understood me?"

His nostrils flared. He sniffed the air and licked the sidewalk. I realized he didn't stop because he understood me. He stopped because he was tracking a scent. Something irresistible.

Hot dogs! He frantically tracked the smell to a hot dog cart. The vendor hollered and hightailed it out of there.

"Hot dogs?" I asked. "You like hot dogs?"

I rushed over and fumbled around the cart. I grabbed as many hot dogs as I could hold and held them out with both hands. The dinosaur came closer. He bent down, and I fed him the hot dogs one at a time. He was careful not to bite my hands. Then he looked me right in the eye. He stared at me for what felt like minutes. Like he was studying me. And in that moment, he imprinted on me. This was a dinosaur in love. I could see it in his eyes. And the weird thing was that the feeling was mutual. But I wasn't ready to accept it yet. He nudged me with his snout, and his stinky hot-dog breath nearly knocked me out.

I said, "Uh-oh. Uh-oh. Look, I am not your mama. No matter how cute you are."

I looked over to see Casey across the street flabbergasted, with her mouth wide open. That marked the first time I had ever seen Casey speechless. In typical form, she was capturing everything on her phone. We looked at each other.

Whoomp! The streets went dark. It was another blackout. Total darkness. At this point, me, Casey, and the dinosaur were the only ones standing in the street. Electrical sparks flashed and rained down. We looked toward the source and saw a glowing blue figure up on the roof of a nearby building.

"*What* is that?" Casey shouted.

I was at the point where the glowing figure scared me and the dinosaur didn't. He was on our side.

"That is why we've been having blackouts," I said. "She's literally stealing our power!"

Meanwhile the dinosaur stayed right by my side.

Suddenly, the glowing figure burst upward in a flash of electrical sparks, knocking a heavy generator off the rooftop.

"Look out!" I yelled as the generator tumbled toward the pavement.

I pointed at Casey and shouted to the dinosaur, "Help her!"

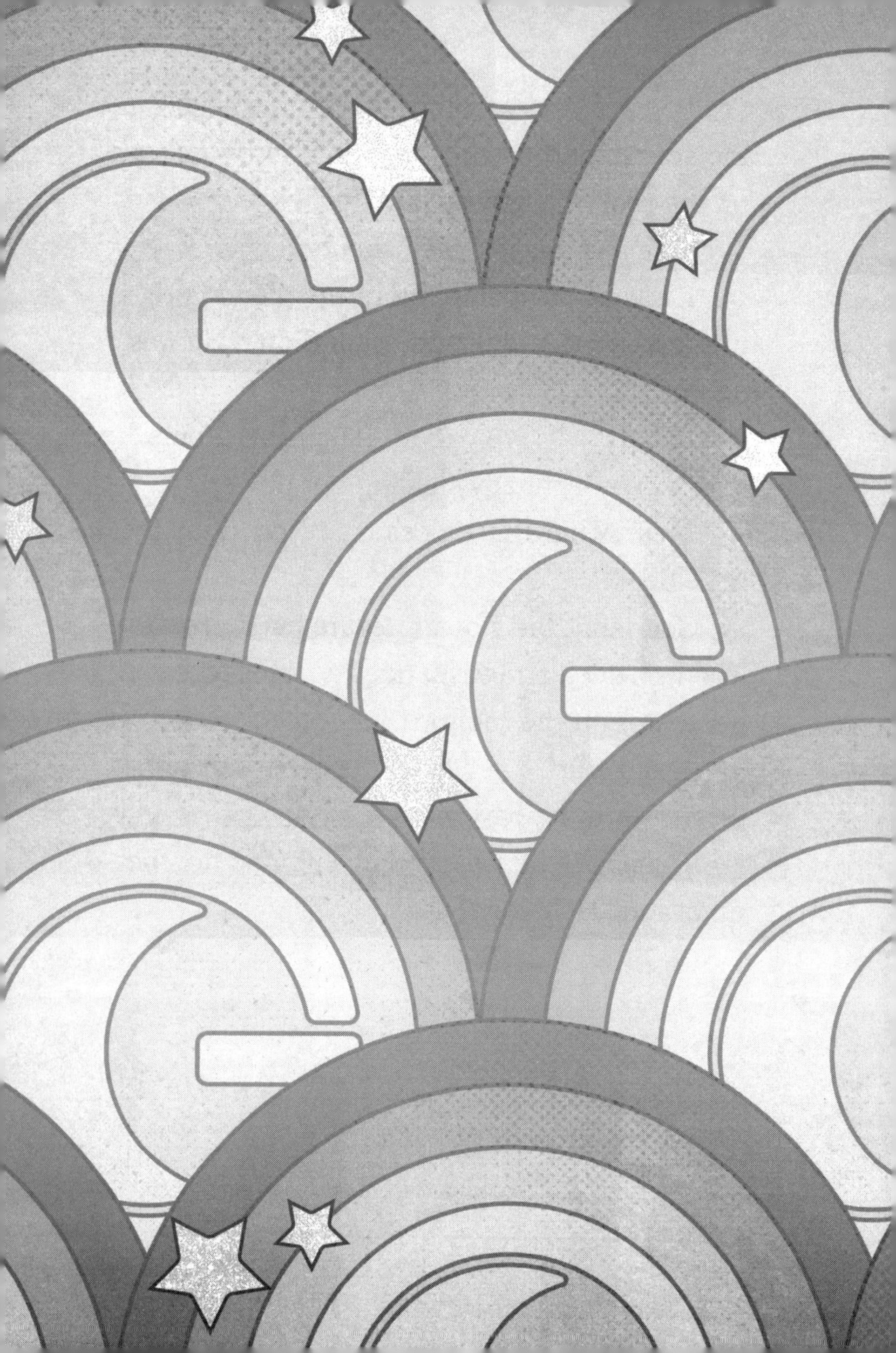

CHAPTER FIVE

In one swift motion, the dinosaur grabbed the generator in his mouth, just seconds before it would have crushed Casey.

I was so relieved that Casey was still alive. I would have felt horrible if that generator had flattened her like a pancake. Miraculously, she still had a tight grip on her phone. I took a step back, and we looked at each other. Casey sat huddled in a ball on the cement. Her face was pale, and she seemed dazed.

She looked fine, but she didn't speak.

I could tell Casey was trying to absorb what had just happened. Sirens wailed and blue lights flashed in the distance. Police cars were heading our way. I wanted to say something to Casey, but the dinosaur and I had to get out of there fast. I remembered a shortcut we could take where we wouldn't be seen.

"C'mon!" I shouted up at the dinosaur. He followed me into a nearby alley. From there, we dashed through more empty alleys and looped back around to the subway tunnel.

"Thank you!" I told him. "I owe you one. You saved Casey's life. I knew your jaws were amazing, but wow! I had no idea they could do all that. That was crazy! Now I just have to figure out what to do with you."

I thought about what my family would say if they saw me with a ten-ton dinosaur. They thought I'd been sound asleep all evening. Would I really be able to hide a dinosaur from them? I wasn't sure, but I was determined to try.

When we got back to the tunnel, I told the dinosaur we had work to do before bedtime. The funny thing was he understood me. I grabbed my tool kit, and we got busy putting the metal grate back in place at the end of the tunnel. The dinosaur picked me up with his tail and plopped me down right on top of his head. From there, I could reach up high, fasten bolts, and secure the grate.

Right above my lab, I created the perfect cozy sleeping spot for a prehistoric creature. I filled it with my biggest stuffed animals and all the extra blankets and pillows I could find.

"How do you like it?" I asked the dinosaur. I stood back and admired my work. "Not bad, right? I promise to come back for you tomorrow morning." I think he approved, because he bumped me with his snout, curled up in a gigantic ball, and went to sleep. He snored softly, a low, steady rumble that reminded me of the sound of our washing machine.

I could barely keep my eyes open. It was times like that when I appreciated my bed-time inventions. One of my devices brushed my teeth without me having to lift a finger. My miniature robot pulled my fuzzy socks out of a bin and brought them to me. As soon as I pulled on my socks, I dropped into bed, wondering if everything that happened that night had been real. I hoped it had.

The next morning, I woke up much earlier than usual. I normally sleep through breakfast, and my mom has to drag me out of bed for school. But I was on a mission. I had to sneak food to a dinosaur without anyone in my family noticing.

Mom, Dad, Pops, and Mimi were all in the kitchen eating breakfast. I slid past them to the fridge, trying to look natural. I mumbled something about needing to take some snacks to school for a study group meeting.

Pops was reading the neighborhood paper.

"Check out this headline," Pops said. "'A Dino Did It'?"

I froze for a second and then kept gathering food.

"I knew it! What have I been telling you for the last forty years?" Pops said.

Mimi said, "You've been saying there are lizards in the sewers and it's only a matter of time before they rise up."

"So a dino could be behind the blackouts, Pops?" Mom said. "Puh-lease. We all know this is about 'the Man' paying no mind to this community."

I was dying to see if there was a picture in the paper, and I was hoping I wasn't in it. I spun around with my arms full of food. I leaned in and took a close look at the paper. The image was a dark silhouette of a dinosaur and a chaotic scene in the street. But it was so dark that none of the people in the picture were identifiable.

"Nuh-uh!" I said. "You're both wrong. A dinosaur didn't cause the blackouts."

They all stared at me.

"Actually—I heard it's some, uh, electrical lady. Sucking up our power. Like an electrical vampire."

Dad, Mom, Pops, and Mimi all burst into laughter.

"Now the lizard uprising sounds legit," Mom said.

Just as I turned to leave, Mimi stopped me.

"What are you doing?" she said. I paused for a second, wondering if I was totally busted. Then Mimi said, "You can't eat all that without taking some of my pie! Here ya go, sweetheart." She added some pie to the top of my stack.

When I got to my lab, the dinosaur heard me coming and stood up. I climbed the staircase to the landing. My makeshift den looked great.

"Good morning!" I said. "Did you miss me?" I stroked the top of his head, and he grunted. He seemed happy to see me. I placed the food down in front of him, and he devoured it in seconds. It made me wonder how often he needed to be fed. He walked around in a circle for a few minutes and settled into a cozy spot. Then he let out a sigh of contentment and a loud burp.

"Pretty dope setup, right? It's an old subway station. I just added a fusion generator, electromagnetic shielding, triple-redundant Internet . . . you know, the basics."

The dinosaur was still hungry, so he got up and followed me down the stairs to my lab. He opened his jaws and started to eat my power generator.

"No, no, not food," I said. "That's what brought you here. It was designed by this super-cool scientist, Moon Girl. She's my hero. Nobody knows her real name. I was trying to replicate her work, and I thought it was a power source, but turns out it rips holes in the space-time continuum. And, well, you were here for the rest.

"You probably wanna get back home. Wherever that is. It's not like I can keep you here . . . right?"

I studied the nuclear fuel gauge on my portal device.

"Your trip here used up half my juice," I said. "And it took forever to synthesize that fuel. There's barely enough to get you home."

The dinosaur extended his tail and curled it around me to pull me closer to him so we could cuddle.

"Does that mean you don't want to go home?" I said, laughing. "What would I even do with you? I can't have you stomping around scaring people like last night. You did save somebody, too. That was crazy, right?"

The dinosaur nodded his head like he was totally following the conversation.

"As if the Lower East Side doesn't have

enough to deal with, and now we have a super villain! What we really need is a super—"

I stopped midsentence because right in that moment, the light bulb inside my head started flashing like crazy.

"Super Heroes! Us! Me and you! With my brains and your brawn, we can really help people." I pictured me and the dinosaur in heroic poses all over the cityscape.

But then I immediately second-guessed the thought. "Whoa, whoa, whoa. Who's going to take a thirteen-year-old Super Hero seriously? But I am the smartest thirteen-year-old I know, and now I have a dinosaur."

The dinosaur grinned proudly. I didn't even think it was possible for a dinosaur to smile. But this dinosaur smiled.

"Oh, but I don't have any super-powers," I continued as I paced back and forth, all excited. "Wait! My brain is my super-power. I can build gadgets—check out my skates. I mean, who else is going to do it? The fate of our community is on the line here, right? So what do you think, big guy? Do you want to be Super Heroes with me?"

The dinosaur smiled and clapped. But I told him we'd have to do this on the DL or my family would freak. "Nobody can know," I said.

Just then, there was a *DING-DONG!*

My home monitor buzzed, and I heard the doorbell ring in the apartment.

"It's a pleasure to finally meet you," someone said. It was a girl's voice.

Mom said, "I'm sorry, sweetheart, and you are?"

"Forgive me. I'm Casey Calderon, Lunella's best friend." That was news to me, but I liked the sound of it.

Dad said, "Lunella Lafayette's best friend?"

I booked it out of the lab as fast as I could. When I joined them in the apartment, Casey was handing out business cards to my parents.

"You have a business card?" Mom asked.

"The paper stock is amazing," Dad said.

"How old are you?" Mom asked.

"Thirteen," Casey said. "But only for now."

I grabbed Casey by the arm.

"Casey! My homie from homeroom. So nice of you to just stop by! Come with me." I whisked Casey away and took her to my bedroom.

"How did you find me?" I asked.

"I found your family's address online. Everything is online! Lunella, I've never seen a bedroom quite like this," Casey said, looking around my room. "What are all of these contraptions?"

"These are my inventions, and the sticky notes—that's all my random brainstorming."

"I brainstorm on sticky notes, too," she said. "Love the crib. Really digging the messy-genius vibe. . . . What's this? Is this one of your inventions, too?" She picked up the strange device my mom had given me.

I grabbed it and put it back down. "No, my mom gave it to me. I have no idea what it is, but I have some ideas about how I might transform it. Look—about what happened last night. Are you going to turn me in?"

Casey said, "Turn you in? What? No way. I came here to thank you for saving my life! I would have been deader than bedazzled denim without you and your big red buddy!"

She looked around.

"Speaking of which, where are you keeping Clifford, anyway?"

I knew she was referring to the dinosaur. I looked at the clock. We still had plenty of time before we had to get to school.

I took a deep breath.

"Can you keep a secret?" I asked.

"Of course!" Casey nodded and grinned from ear to ear.

I locked my bedroom door.

"Follow me," I said, heading for my closet. Casey looked puzzled.

I had never shown anyone my lab before. Ever. But I felt like it was now or never. I figured I had to share my secrets with somebody.

After all, now I had two best friends—Casey and a *T. rex*.

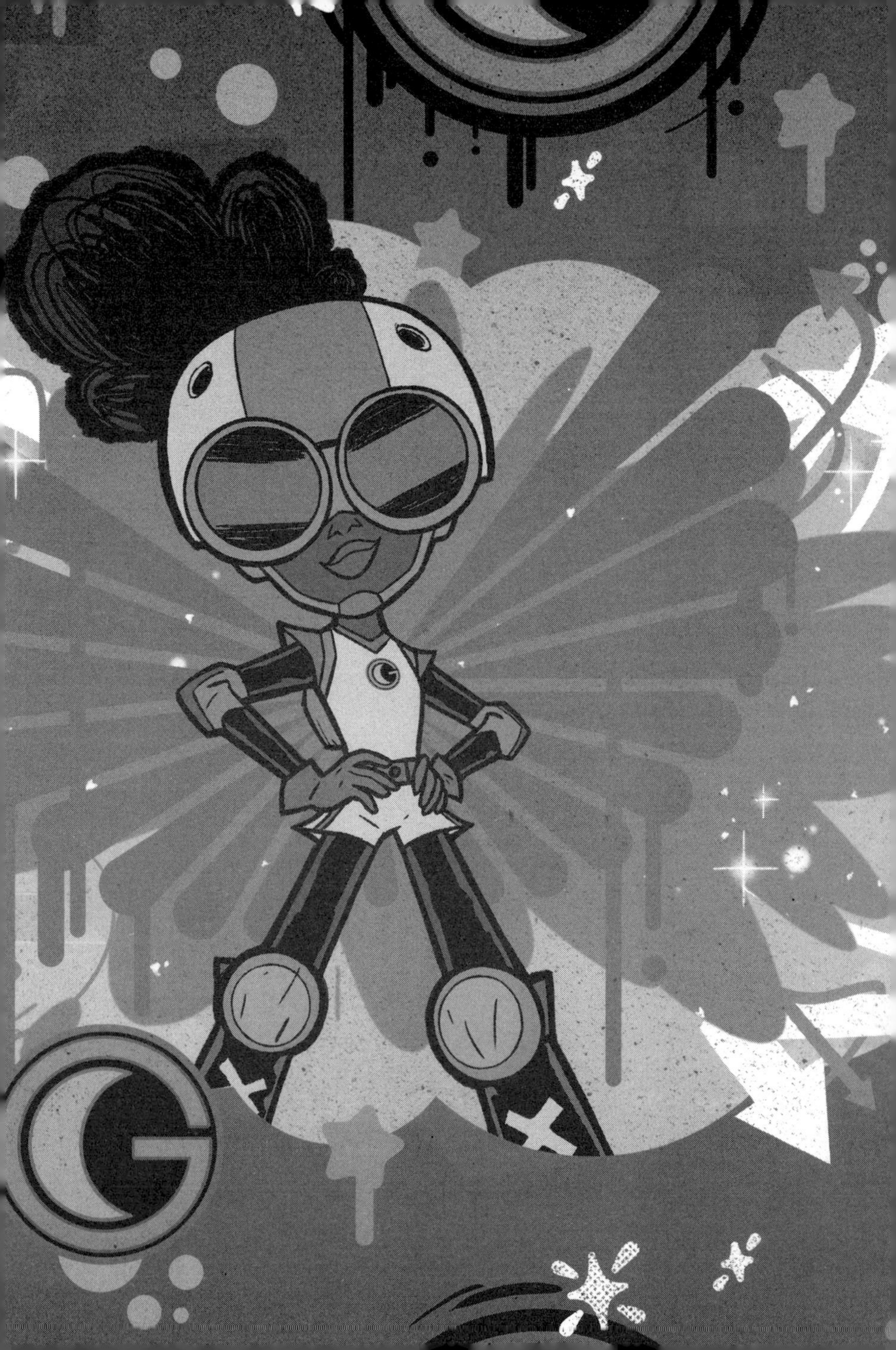

CHAPTER SIX

"I don't get it," **Casey said** as we walked into my closet. She ran her fingers across my T-shirts. "And by the way, I could do a lot with this closet. You could use some brighter colors in your wardrobe. What are we doing in here?"

"You'll see," I said.

When I tugged on the pull string, my closet shook and rumbled as it transformed into an elevator car.

Casey grabbed my arm.

When the elevator doors opened, we stepped into my lab.

"En serio?" Casey said. "You built all this?" Her eyes grew wide, and she started wandering around.

"The dino is over here," I said, pointing to the windows overlooking the lab. "I made him a den." Casey followed me up the stairs.

The dinosaur was fast asleep. Casey leaned in to get a closer look at his face. When he snored loudly, she jumped back.

"Don't worry," I whispered. "He won't hurt us. I actually think he loves me. And it's not only because I gave him hot dogs. I feel a real connection with him. Does that sound completely crazy?"

"Maybe a little crazy, but I think it's fantastic!"

Casey lifted up her phone and snapped a few photos of the dinosaur. Then she took photos of the lab from different angles.

"This is so unbelievable," she whispered.

"If I wasn't seeing all of this with my own eyes, I would never believe it."

"You know you can't post those photos anywhere, right? This is supposed to be my *secret* lab."

"I promise I won't post them. I just want documentation for us. For our records." I hoped she was telling the truth.

Then she turned to me and said, "Okay, I need to know how this happened. Every. Single. Detail."

As soon as we got back downstairs, I took a deep breath and let it all out.

"See, it all started with my hero: Moon Girl." I showed Casey Moon Girl's picture hanging on the wall. I told her how I had tried to replicate her work, which meant I re-created her power source. I had the designs all worked out in my engineering notebook. I grabbed it and waved it around in the air. "See, this is why I love engineering. Because it's all about solving problems, and with all the power outages that have been happening, I was trying to solve problems for the Lower East Side. But turns out it's not actually a power source. It's a portal generator. And next thing I know, a giant dinosaur came through the portal. He just came strutting into my lab and started running around the city and—"

I paused and gasped for air. It was such a relief to unload! It reminded me of the time when I took apart all the cell phones in our apartment because I wanted to compare them and see how they worked. Mom, Dad, Mimi, and Pops were going wild looking for their phones—they all thought they had lost them—because it took me a few days to put them back together. I finally had to fess up, and it was a relief to tell them the truth.

I heard the dinosaur snorting. "I think he's waking up," I said.

Casey followed me back up the steps. He was wide awake. He sniffed Casey, and then he sniffed me.

"You remember Casey, right?" I slid an artificial bone across the floor to him. "Check out this bone I made with my 3D printer."

"Wow!" Casey said. "It looks so real."

The dinosaur tossed the bone around with his snout for a few seconds, and then he gnawed on it.

I told Casey my idea about how me and the dinosaur could be Super Heroes and protect the LES from the electric lady.

"The fate of our community is on the line here. And there's no one else who can do it. We have to do it!" I said.

Casey and the dinosaur stared at me.

"Besides . . . Mom always says, 'One girl can make a difference.'"

I finally stopped pacing. I felt myself standing taller. I felt empowered. Like I really could save the world, or at least the Lower East Side.

"So whaddaya think?" I looked at Casey.

"About you being a Super Hero?" Casey asked.

"Yeah!"

"No."

"*What?* But I thought you liked the idea."

"Not in that outfit. No client of mine is going out like that," Casey said.

"Client?" I said. "And what's wrong with my outfit?" I looked down at my clothes. I was wearing what I always wore that time of year—black T-shirt, jeans, black sneakers.

"Yes, a client. I can provide full-service management and public relations. I can turn you into the most beloved Super Heroes in the world! I'm talkin' digital marketing, viral videos, personal appearances, merchandising opportunities—this lab is going to make a great play set."

"My lab? A play set? Girl, have you lost your mind?"

Casey said, "I've been told that I can be a bit much, but honestly, I don't see it. Look, I can tell you're gonna inspire people, just like you inspired me. I can get your message out there. I can help you help people. And you don't have to pay me a cent. Social media followers are my currency."

"That's a lot to take in," I said. "Aight, let's do this thing!"

Casey said, "First things first. Costume. I'm thinking Iron Man, but less subtle. Full automation. Artificial intelligence, Wi-Fi, jet pack, surround sound, color-changing LEDs depending on your mood."

"Lovin' everything you're saying. Just one problem. Who's got Iron Man money?"

"Oh, right," Casey said.

"But like we do around here," I told Casey, "we just gotta roll with it! I'm going to scrounge for materials around the neighborhood, and I'll make my own stuff."

Casey and I decided to meet back at my apartment after school the next day to finalize my costume and gear. That gave me time to make a plan for gathering materials. And I knew where my first stop would be.

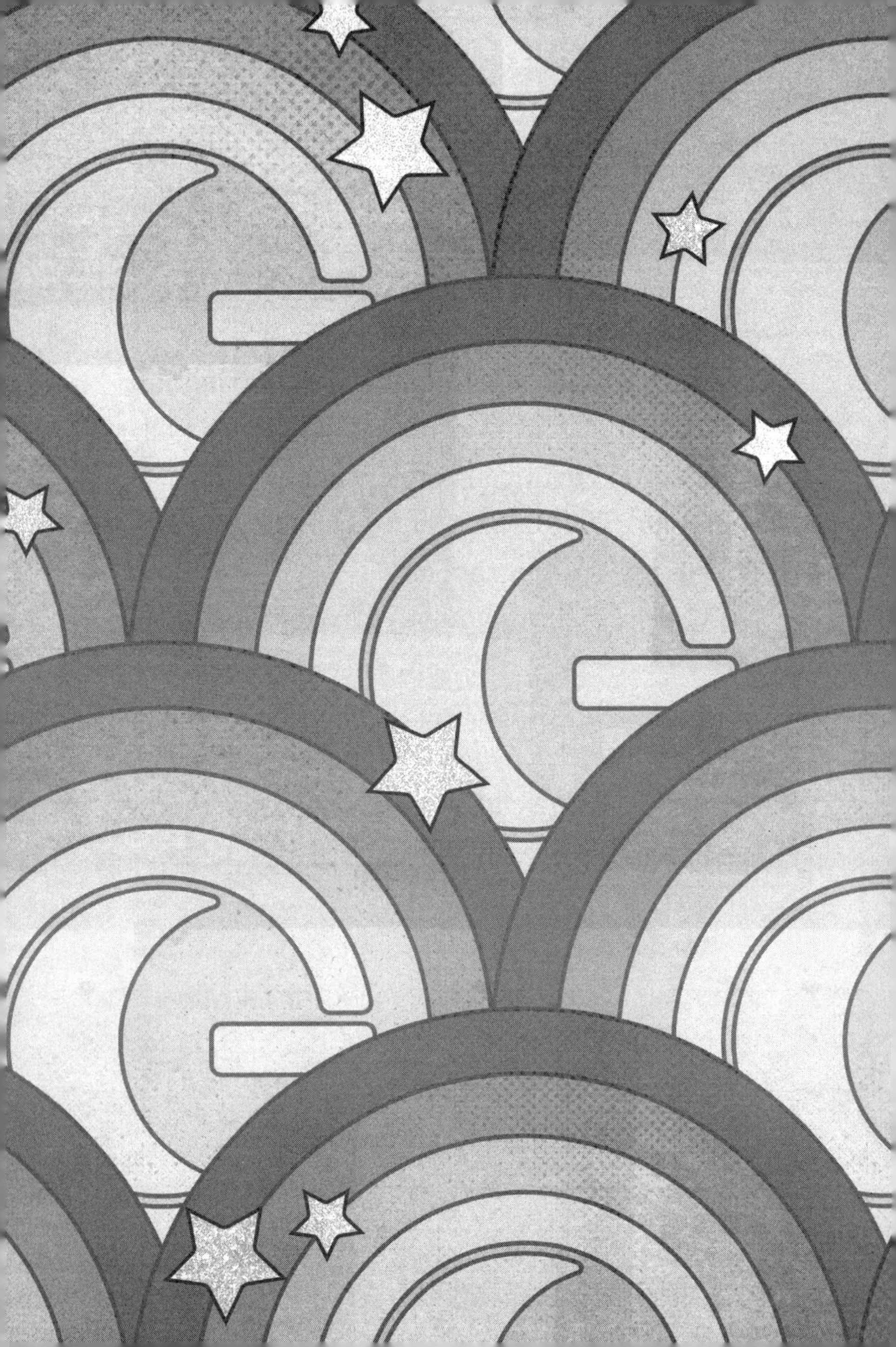

CHAPTER SEVEN

● ●

When I rolled into Mr. Septimus's pawn shop, he was crouched down on the floor reaching for an outlet.

"Hi, Mr. Septimus!" I said. "Let me help you with that. I can reach it. Even in roller skates, I can get down low." Mr. Septimus had unplugged all his equipment during a blackout earlier. The power had just come back on, so I helped him plug everything back in.

There were three reasons Mr. Septimus's

pawn shop was my first stop. For one, he inspires me. Over the years, he has taught me a lot. He tells amazing stories about up-cycling, which means transforming something in a way that makes it better and more useful. Some of his stories have sparked new ideas for my inventions. And now he calls me the Queen of Upcycling. The second reason was because after I helped Mr. Septimus automate his inventory last year, he started saving old electronics and spare parts for me to use in my lab. And the third reason is because Mr. Septimus always tells me straight up what's going on in our neighborhood—no sugarcoating. He told me a couple more LES shops had gone out of business because of the blackouts, just like Bubbe Bina's Knish Niche. And he said even when shops stayed open, the blackouts slowed down their operations.

"When the computers don't work, I have to ring people up the old-fashioned way," Mr. Septimus explained as he dropped electronics into a cardboard box for me. "I have to write down what the customer purchased and the credit card information. Cash is easier to deal with. But whether it's cash or a credit card, I still have to spend time entering all the sales into the computer manually when the electricity comes back on. It's the only way to keep my inventory and my money up to date."

I wanted so badly to tell him about the electric lady and how I planned to make sure the blackouts stopped happening. But I just said, "Well, I hope the power gets fixed soon."

"Will you be able to carry all this?" he asked, placing the box in my arms.

"I'll be fine," I told him. "Thanks for everything." Some magnetic sensors and remote controls spilled out of the box, and I stuffed them into my backpack.

By the time I left the pawn shop, I was more determined than ever to make things right for the LES. I felt like I could upcycle anything. I hit up Jimmy's Gym and got my hands on a boxing glove and knee pads. I dug through the lost and found at Roll With It and found an old roller derby jersey and helmet.

Back in the lab, I showed the dinosaur the goodies I'd found in the dumpster behind Señora Martinez's bodega.

"You know I hooked you up!" I told him as I dumped loaves of bread on the floor. "You can chomp on this while I work." Then I played hip-hop, because it always gets my creative juices flowing. The dinosaur liked hip-hop, too. In fact, I figured out it was his favorite because, of all the music I had been playing, his tail thumped the fastest during hip-hop. I could have sworn this dinosaur was dancing!

The next day, after school, Casey showed up at our apartment with her sewing machine and Puerto Rican *arroz con pollo* (aka chicken and rice). So yummy! After we ate, Casey worked her magic on the old roller derby jersey. I was impressed with how she cut, sewed, and applied sequins. She made the jersey look cute, sparkly, and totally new. So I wasn't the only one who knew how to upcycle material.

"You're really talented," I told her.

I liked hanging out with Casey more than I thought I would. As different as we seemed, we had a lot in common. We both loved eating spicy food, dancing to hip-hop, creating new things, asking a zillion questions, and making a difference in our community. I told her about my family and the roller rink, and she told me all about her *papis*, Isaac and Antonio. When I told Casey how Pops taught me how to turn regular shoes into roller skates, she said that's kind of like how Antonio taught her all about color schemes.

While Casey focused on her fashion projects, I put the finishing touches on my inventions and gave Casey demonstrations. She seemed truly interested in my lab. She wanted to know all sorts of things, like the difference between the scientific method and the engineering design process.

"As your manager and BFF," Casey said, "the more I understand what you do, the more I can help you."

"Well, when I use the scientific method, I ask questions, conduct experiments, test hypotheses, analyze data, and draw conclusions," I told her. "For the engineering design process, I still do a lot of research, but it's more about defining a problem, specifying requirements, and developing and testing solutions with a prototype, which is like an early model of my product."

"So are you a scientist or an engineer?" Casey asked.

"Both!" I said. "I love it all. Science and engineering go together like partners. Science helps me understand the world. And I like to take what I learn from science and use it to create cool technology.

"Check this out," I said as I hooked wires

to my boxing glove and hit a switch. The glove shrank to fit my hand just like a normal glove. And when I hit the switch again, it expanded back to full size in a fraction of a second.

"It's like a magic trick!" Casey said.

"It is kind of like magic," I said. "Compressed air and expanding foam! And thanks to Mr. Septimus's spare parts, I also made these tricked-out goggles. I even connected them to my phone. I can read every text you send me with these goggles if I want."

"That's why you borrowed my phone earlier! And how about the emojis? Did you figure that out?"

"Yup," I said. "These emojis reflect my mood by sensing my heart rate and body heat."

Every now and then, the dinosaur peeked through the window to see what we were doing.

"*Voilà!*" Casey said as she held up my

jersey. I pulled on my new costume and demonstrated how the wheels popped out of the bottoms of my boots. Then Casey dug around in a big pink backpack that she called her tool bag. I thought that was funny because her tool bag is filled with safety pins, sewing needles, thread, fabric, hair products, flavored lip glosses, and other cosmetics. My tool bag is filled with wrenches, screwdrivers, pliers, wire cutters, bolts, cords, and electronic device parts. Both bags of tools are useful, just in different ways.

"Hold still," Casey said. "This jersey is still a little too big." She pinned the jersey back on both sides. She pressed and tucked and pinned more until it fit just right.

Then I slicked my hair up into one big Afro puff, which fit perfectly through my helmet.

Casey circled me, nodding approvingly. She held up a mirror in front of me. Then she snapped pictures of me, and we looked at them together.

"Daaaang! We did the thang-thang," I said.

Casey said, "Yup. I can sell this. Just the last little detail: what's your Super Hero name?"

"Name? Do I really need one?"

"Yes. If you don't take yourself seriously, no one else will. Super Skater Sister and her Savage Salamander!" Casey said.

"Um, no, not feelin' that—let's think on this some more."

Even though I didn't have a Super Hero name at that point, I felt like we were ready for action. We left the lab, and I led the dinosaur down a quiet street in the dark. Casey was right behind us, filming.

"So until we can locate that power-sucking electrical lady," I said, "the best we can do for now is stop blackout crime in its tracks."

Just then, the lights flickered. Another blackout.

"Like right now!" I said. Glass shattered, but we couldn't tell where the sound came from. We screamed and clung to each other behind a bus shelter.

I tapped my goggles and switched to night vision. I looked all around trying to figure out what had shattered. Through the goggles, I saw two burglars across the street inside Loco Louie's Discount Electronics. They had broken the front window and were looting the place.

"It's the same fools who tried to rob Roll With It!" I said.

"How do you know?" Casey asked.

"Because my homemade security system at the rink sprayed blue dye all over this guy's face. And I can see his face is still blue."

"A robbery in progress?" Casey said. "What do we do? What do we do?"

"Uh, we're already doing recon, so that's a start. I think we should wait for them to come out of the shop. Then somehow we need to attack them while you capture it all on video and make us famous?"

Casey lifted her phone and put on her wireless headset.

"Yeah, let's do that," she said. "And totally unrelated: my hands are shaking."

"My everything is shaking," I said. "But my grandma Mimi once told me bravery is what you do when you're flat-out scared."

"Old people are the best," Casey said.

"As Mimi would say, 'Ain't that the truth.' Now let's do this."

When the burglars came out of the shop, they had dollies loaded up with stolen goods.

And that's when I realized I didn't quite know what you're supposed to say when you're trying to stop criminals.

"Uh, stop right there!" I called out.

One of the burglars paused and looked in our direction. For a split second, I thought about telling Casey to forget this whole Super Hero thing. Maybe there was time for us to run.

But it was too late. One of the burglars was heading straight for me.

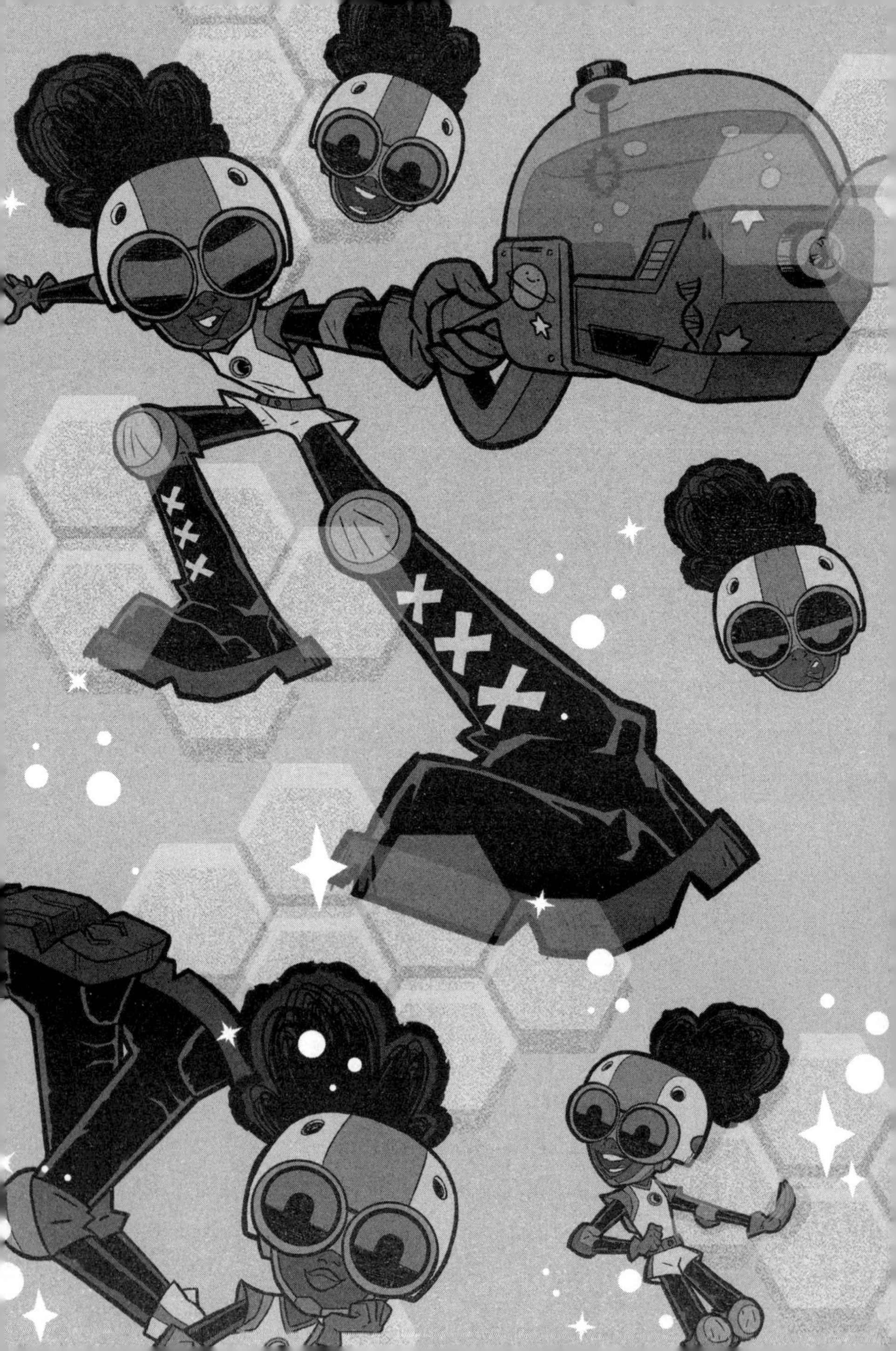

CHAPTER EIGHT

. . . .

The burglar got right up in my face, and I
took a step back.

"And you are?" He smirked and looked
me up and down.

"Uh, my name's TBD," I said.

"No offense, but TBD's a terrible name."

"No, TBD is not my name. TBD means 'to
be determined,' and why am I explaining this?
All you need to know is that I'm a Super Hero,
my turf is the LES, and you're messin' with it."

"You? A Super Hero?" he said, laughing. "And you don't even have a name? If you don't take yourself seriously, no one will."

"That's what I said," Casey chimed in.

"Not helping," I said, turning in Casey's direction.

"Sorry!" Casey said.

I wondered if it was possible to literally die from humiliation. I can't stand to be laughed at, and this guy thought I was hilarious. Whenever kids make fun of me at school, I'm an expert at ignoring them. But that wasn't an option here. My only hope was that my dinosaur had my back.

"I bet my friend will make you take me seriously!" I pointed behind me.

"Who? The gym guy?" The burglar looked confused.

When I turned around, the only thing I saw behind me was the guy in the Jimmy's Gym ad on the bus shelter.

"Hold up, where did he go?" I said. Casey

shrugged. I didn't see the dinosaur, but I heard him. I followed the sounds of gobbling. Casey followed me and kept filming. Even the burglar seemed curious about who I was looking for. I found the dino with his head inside a dumpster! He was chowing down on who knows what.

"For real?" I said. "You have to do this right now?" The dinosaur looked up at me like he didn't have a care in the world. He walked over and licked my face.

"Uck, dumpster mouth!" I said. Then he burped. Casey held her nose. Whatever he was eating smelled worse than rotten eggs. Back at the lab, I had been testing out a new formula to make the dino's breath smell better. I made a mental note to fast-track that project.

"See those two bad guys?" I said to the dinosaur. "I need you to go get 'em—as in, attack!"

At this point, the burglars calmly strolled

by us, wheeling their stolen goods. I reached out with both arms and grabbed the dinosaur's tail.

"I need you to come help me!" I shouted. But he thought I was playing a game. He started running in circles. Which might not have been so bad if I hadn't still been holding on to his tail. I spun around and around in the air so many times I felt dizzy.

"It's not playtime!" I yelled. The dinosaur rolled on his back, and the burglars dumped their final load into their truck. Then they drove over to where me and Casey were standing and rolled down a window.

"So yeah," said one of the burglars. "We're gonna leave now. But keep up the good work, dino. Blackouts are great for business!"

"Crime is wrong!" I shouted. I know it sounded silly, but it was all I could think of. I wanted to try something to keep them from getting away. In a last-ditch effort, I thrust my boxing glove toward the open truck window. The good news was when I clicked it, the glove inflated and fired off my hand. But the bad news was the dinosaur bumped me with his tail and knocked me down, so my aim was totally off. The glove flew right past the burglars and to the side. *Wham!* It crashed into Casey's phone. The phone flew out of her hand and landed across the street.

"Noooooo!" Casey yelled.

"Good luck with all the Super Hero stuff!" said the burglar as he leaned out of the window. As they drove off, we could hear them howling with laughter. Casey scrambled to pick up her phone and then rushed over to me.

"It's okay! Don't worry," Casey said. "My phone is fine. But I am definitely deleting this video. Are you okay?"

"I'm okay," I said as Casey helped me off the ground. I felt sick to my stomach. Was it from the dinosaur spinning me around in the air, or was it from the mortifying humiliation? I wasn't sure.

"I want a do-over!" I told Casey. "This didn't go like I thought it would. We need a strategic planning meeting. We need to regroup."

"Strategic planning is one of my specialties," Casey said.

Back in the lab, I paced back and forth while Casey took notes in a sparkly pink notebook. Even the dinosaur was pacing.

"If I don't clean up this crime, the LES is gonna keep going downhill, my parents are gonna have to sell the rink, and next thing ya know, I'm moving to Jersey! No disrespect to Jersey."

Casey said, "Course not. Great beaches, Bruce Springsteen, saltwater taffy—but you're a New York City girl. We can't let that happen. I won't let that happen."

"Thanks, Casey." It meant a lot to me that she cared. We brainstormed a checklist of things we needed to work on, like how far away Casey should be standing when she was filming and how we could make sure the dinosaur didn't wander off right in the middle of all the action.

"And I have another idea," I said. "Your part involves some high-level messing around on the Internet."

"That's every day of my life," Casey said. "What are you gonna do?"

"All the best Super Heroes need training," I said. "Meet us back here on Saturday. We need time to get this super team in super sync." And I knew the perfect training ground.

Me and the dinosaur spent time training in Seward Park at night. We went over basic commands like sit, roll over, stop, stay, fetch. Hot dogs were my training tools. I flung a garbage can lid across the park. The dinosaur retrieved it and picked up a hot dog. The tricky part was training him to pay attention and stay focused on a task when food was around. So we practiced a "leave it—don't eat it!" command. It was hard for him, but we made progress. We practiced weaving and bobbing and attacking. The dinosaur weaved through the swings and jumped over the slide. His tail whipped a criminal. Well, it was really a fake criminal I'd made out of branches and garbage.

The dinosaur watched while I practiced using my fighting devices. I fired my boxing gloves at a row of cans on a seesaw. After each glove flew free, another inflated on my hand. One after the other, the cans fell. Perfect strikes!

After our last training session, we ate chocolate ice cream on a rooftop overlooking the city. I looked away for two seconds, and the dinosaur snatched my ice cream cone with his tongue.

"Seriously? As Bubbe Bina would say, you're a real bandit, y'know that?"

He grunted. He was asking me a question.

"Oh," I said. "A bandit means like a rascal,

like someone who is devilish. Hey, what's your name, anyway?"

He grunted a loooong name, and I understood him. He'd said his name was Terrifying Fire Beast Who Will Bring About the End of All Things.

"Okay, that will not fit on a T-shirt," I said. "So let's shorten it. I'm calling you Devil Dinosaur."

He grunted with approval.

"At least one of us has a name," I said.

On Saturday in the lab, Casey pulled a piece of paper out of her backpack and slapped it down on the table in front of me. There was an address written on it.

"BAM!" she said. "Thanks to my mad Internet skills, I found the auction site listing for all the stolen goods. *Esos tontos* are trying to auction all the stolen stuff on the web. I snagged their address."

"Yes!" I said. "That's lit, Casey!"

"So, what have you been up to?" she said.

"I trained a predator, mastered my fighting devices, whipped up a new device, and, oh, I speak fluent dinosaur now. And guess what? I finally know his name."

"Please tell me it's brand-friendly," Casey said.

"Well, the literal translation is Terrifying Fire Beast Who Will Bring About the End of All Things."

Casey looked like she might hyperventilate.

"Buuut, good news—we discussed it, and we're going to go with Devil Dinosaur for short."

"Devil?" Casey said. "Short and catchy. Yeah, I can work with that."

We used a fake email address to make arrangements with the burglars. We pretended to be customers interested in buying their stolen goods.

"We get a do-over tomorrow night!" I said. Me and Casey danced around the lab and chanted over and over: "We found you. We found you. We're going to the big baddies' hideout!"

I just knew this time had to be different. We were trained and ready, *right*? Plus I had perfected a new device called the Bubble Blaster.

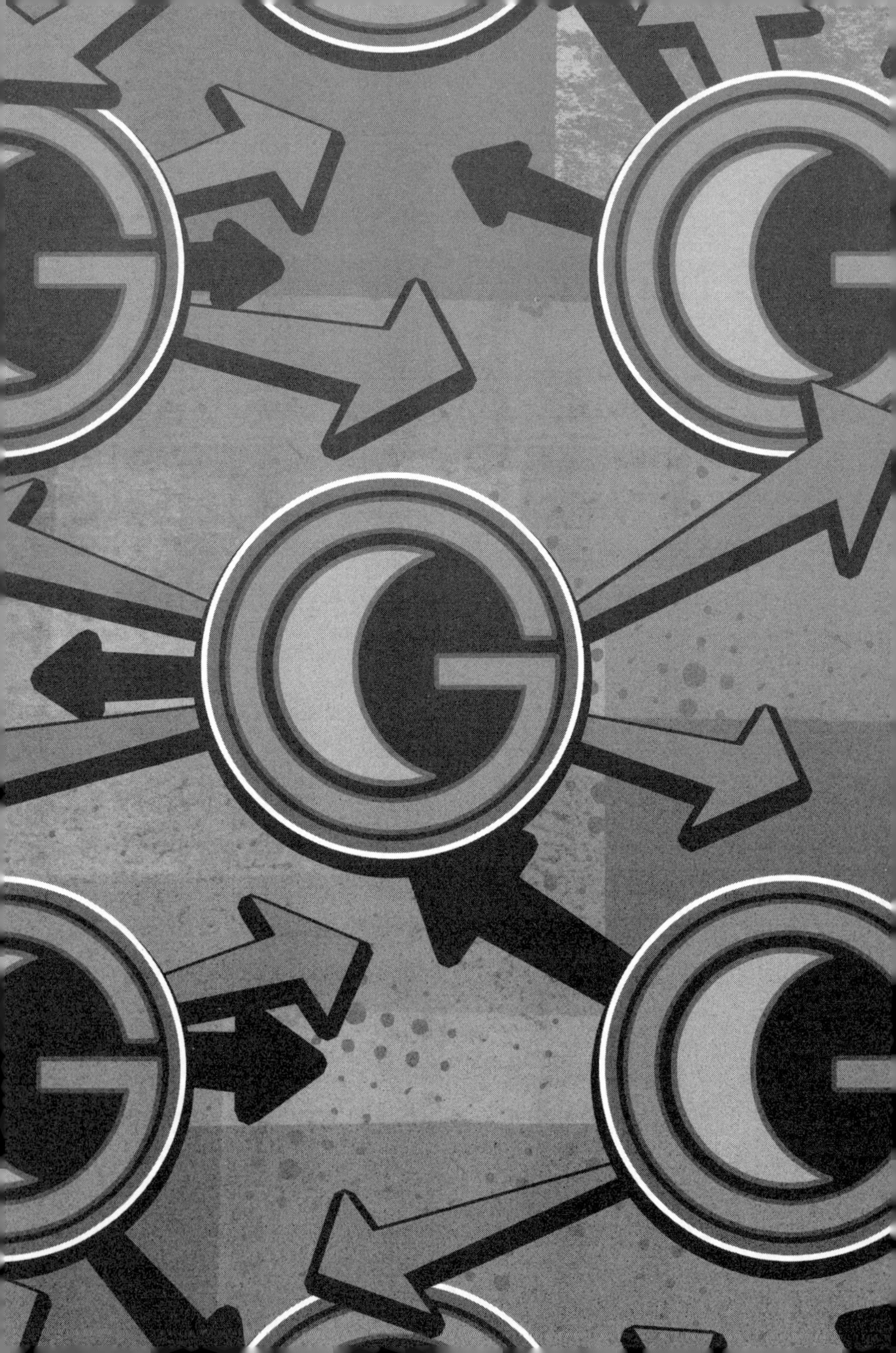

CHAPTER NINE

With Casey and Devil Dinosaur on my side, I felt like I had two besties. It was the first time I'd ever had friends who weren't grown-ups. And I learned a lot about both of them in a short amount of time.

On Sunday, Casey came over early so we could discuss some research before heading to the big baddies' hideout. Casey wanted to show me her Super Hero branding ideas, including a proposed schedule for crime fighting that would get maximum viewership on social media. I told her crime doesn't exactly happen on such a planned schedule, but I admired her organizational skills. She had extensive data about social media and marketing trends, and I loved her knack for segmenting audiences and identifying patterns.

Casey appreciated my research, too. Ever since Devil arrived, I had been collecting and analyzing data on various aspects of his intelligence and behavior. All my tests confirmed that he was super smart. And I showed Casey digital pie charts displaying his favorite activities; painting with his tail and watching monster movies were at the top of the list. He especially liked *Godzilla* and *Creature from the Black Lagoon*. I also identified Devil's dislikes with bar graphs. He was not a fan of jellyfish or clowns. They totally freaked him out.

As soon as it got dark outside, me and Casey suited up while we listened to music. I buckled my helmet, snapped my goggles, and poofed my Afro puff. Casey tweezed her eyebrows, brushed her bangs, and put on lip gloss. While I holstered the Bubble Blaster, Casey holstered her phone.

After we finished going over our entire checklist, I said, "We covered everything. I think we're ready."

"And remember," Casey said, grabbing both of my shoulders, "you weren't defeated by those robbers. You're about to have an epic comeback!"

"Let's go get 'em!" I said.

When we got to the big baddies' hideout, we peeked through an open window. It was a huge warehouse. The two burglars sat at a table. They were surrounded by radios, televisions, laptops, computer monitors, and other stolen electronics. There was a large platter with slices of ham, turkey, bologna, and salami. Ahmed's cold cuts!

One of the burglars chomped on a sandwich while the other one dabbed powder on his face. Unfortunately for him, I'd made sure that blue dye wouldn't fade for weeks.

It was a perfect time for me to make an entrance. I busted through the door.

"Oh, it's little miss Super Hero without a name," said the blue-faced burglar. "Are you back for more humiliation?"

"Well, there is one name I picked." I whistled and yelled, "Devil!"

Right on cue, Devil shoved his head through the door and let out a *ROARRRRRR!* The warehouse floor shook as Devil smashed a hole right through the wall. As Devil stomped toward them, the burglars jumped out of their seats and scrambled backward. Then they ran.

One burglar ran in my direction, so I fired off my boxing glove, and *BAM!* I hit him right in the jaw. He dropped to the ground.

"Owwww!" he said.

"I've been practicing," I said. Then I looked at Devil and pointed to the burglar. "Fetch!" I yelled.

Devil scampered after the burglar. He snagged him by the back of his shirt and lifted him in the air.

"Hey!" yelled the burglar.

"Attaboy!" I said.

Devil trotted back to me with the burglar dangling from his mouth. Then, suddenly, Devil stopped and sniffed the air. Uh-oh—I recognized that look on his face. He whipped his head toward the source of the smell: cold cuts.

"Devil . . . leave it," I said. "Leave it and don't eat it!" Sweat oozed from his scales. His jaw trembled. Saliva dripped from his mouth all over the burglar.

"Yuck!" yelled the burglar. I felt sorry for him, but only for a second.

"Listen, leave it!" I ordered. "Leave it! Don't eat it!"

The burglar said, "Look at these yummy cold cuts. Mmmmmmm. Meat good."

"You got this, Devil D," I said. "Leave it!"

Devil looked at me. Then his tail whipped the cold cut platter to the ground, and he growled.

"Yes!" I said. "I knew you could stay strong."

"Guys!" Casey said, racing over to us. "The one who never talks is getting away!"

The second burglar was sneaking out the big hole in the wall. We were about to chase him when Devil stopped. He lowered his head in front of me, and I climbed on his back.

We headed down a side street. Casey ran alongside us, filming the entire time. Sometimes she sent me text messages that I could read with my goggles. Devil galloped down the street with a burglar still dangling from his jaw. I concentrated on staying steady and not falling off, just like we practiced. As we closed in on the burglar who was running away, I grabbed the Bubble Blaster. I aimed it at the burglar, held as still as I could, and *BLOOP!* The device released a gigantic bubble. It floated through the air and enveloped the burglar's whole body.

"Got 'iiim!" I said. I had worked up a formula that made the bubble smell like fruity bubble gum. I thought about making the bubbles stinky. But the problem with that is it wouldn't be stinky only for the person trapped in the bubble. It would be stinky for anyone in the vicinity, including me. So I went with a fruity smell.

"I'm definitely not deleting this video," Casey said.

Suddenly, we heard crackling. Streaks of light flashed across the sky. Then a glowing blue figure came into view on top of a nearby building.

"The electrical lady!" me and Casey both said in unison. She was sucking up power as usual. She turned toward us.

"Hey, hey, hey!" she said. "My name ain't Electrical Lady. It's Aftershock." Then she looked at me and squeed.

"Ohhhh, look at you! That cosplay is adorbs. Who are you supposed to be?"

I thought: *Here we go again. Another person laughing at me.*

"I'm . . ." Then I paused because I remembered I didn't have a Super Hero name yet.

One of the burglars said, "See?"

I wanted to shout, "I get it! I'll pick a name soon." But instead I said to the burglar, "Don't even start with me. And the cops are on their way. They're coming for you."

Aftershock said to me, "M'kay, you work on that name. Gotta jet. I do have a day job— that's right, a gal can do it all. *Byeeee.*" She flew off, laughing. Pure evil.

As soon as we saw that the cops had captured the burglars and knew the location of the warehouse, we booked it back to the lab. While Devil tossed a truck tire around, I paced back and forth. Yes, we got the burglars. But Aftershock was still out there.

"C'mon," Casey said. "Enjoy the win, will

ya? The big takeaway is we Super-Heroed! And don't stress about your name. We'll sleep on it. Maybe do some guided meditation."

Just then I stopped in my tracks. The photo of Moon Girl caught my attention. I stared at it for a few seconds.

"Moon Girl!" I said. "That's my name. I'm gonna be Moon Girl. She's my hero! My biggest inspiration."

"And Moon Girl is short and catchy—easy to remember and easy to say," Casey said. "I like it!"

I jumped in the air and gave Devil a high five.

"Moon Girl and Devil Dinosaur!" I shouted.

Casey leaned over and whispered, "And Casey!" Then we did a fancy fist bump. Because that's what you do when you're an unstoppable trio! Casey showed me all the likes the Bubble Blaster video was racking up on social media.

"And check out my latest invention. I'm

going to call it the Multispectrum Moon Scanner," I said. "I finally figured out that this old thing my mom gave me is a cassette player. She used it to listen to music when she was younger. It still plays music, but I turned it into a scanner with multiple capabilities." The scanner beeped as I demonstrated the functionality. "I added circuits right here and a screen. Now this device can analyze particles, detect signals, project energy, and best of all—track villains."

We updated our mission with markers on a big whiteboard:

• Stop Aftershock.

• Stop the blackouts.

• Save the LES.

"But first we gotta find her," I said, raising the Moon Scanner in the air.

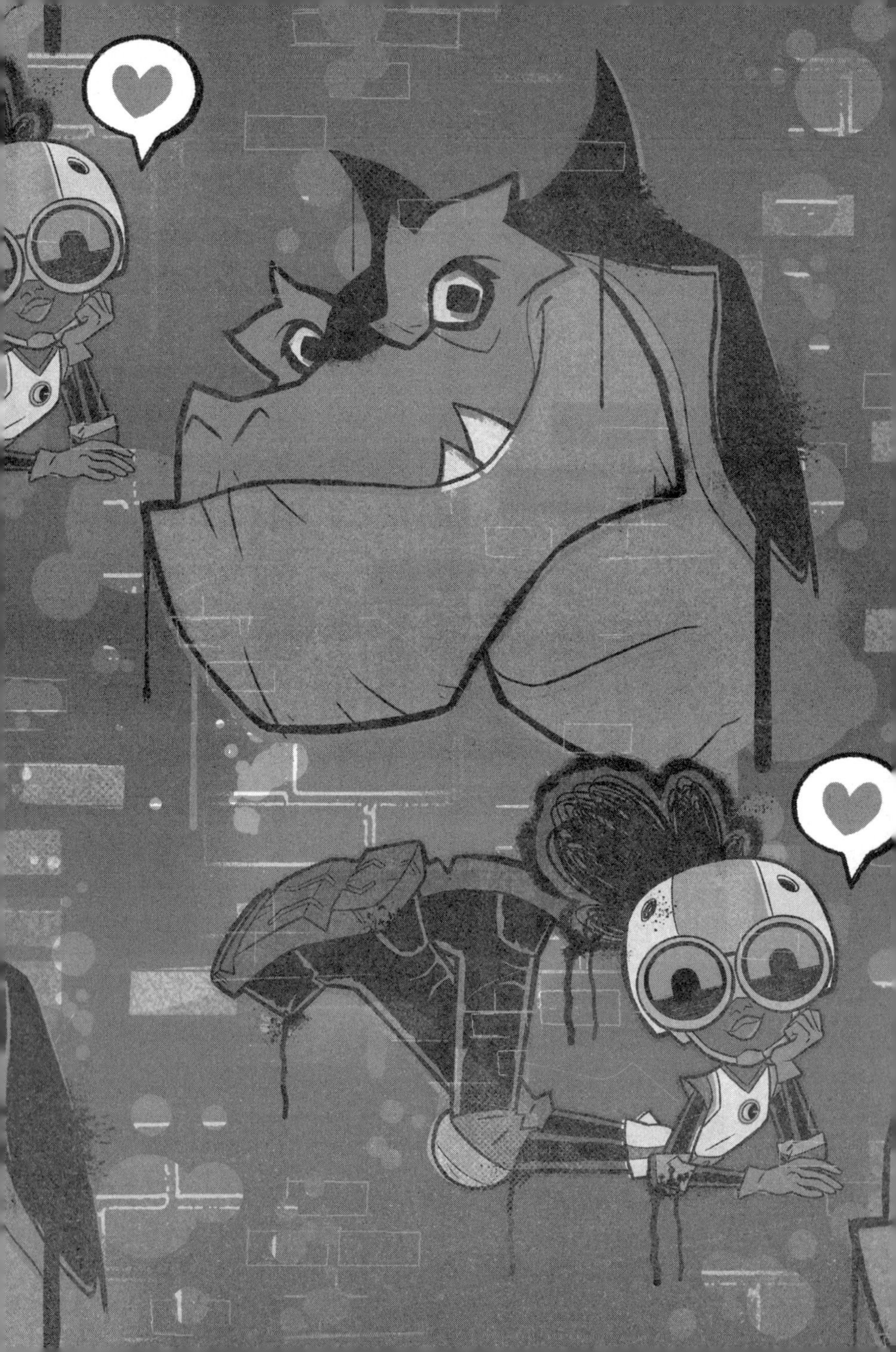

CHAPTER TEN

One of my favorite things about having a dinosaur is being able to talk with him about everything. I've told Devil Dinosaur things I would never tell anybody else. And Devil always tells me he understands where I'm coming from, and he doesn't think I'm an awful person for saying certain things out loud. Like when I told him I hoped Casey would never have another friend that she liked better than me. Devil said he hoped I would never leave him for another dinosaur that I liked better than him.

I also admitted to Devil that I was totally pooped. Part of my exhaustion came from taking care of a dinosaur at all hours of the night, but I didn't mention that part because I didn't want to hurt his feelings. Plus I loved taking care of him. But I told him about all the other stuff that was wearing me out. It was a good thing it took me only fifteen minutes every night to do all my homework for school. Because along with caring for Devil, I was juggling my boxing lessons at Jimmy's Gym, my job fixing things at the roller rink, and all my science experiments and inventions, which were in various stages of development.

And that was on top of everything else we were doing to take down criminals and perform community outreach in the LES while we kept looking for Aftershock with the Moon Scanner. One day in front of Loco

Louie's Discount Electronics, I rode on Devil's back while Devil unloaded crates from a flatbed truck for Louie. Louie said it was the most exciting thing that had ever happened to him in his whole life. Just as Casey planned, the videos of us helping different LES shop owners went viral. We started a new hashtag: #MoonGirlMagic.

At school on Monday, I dozed off in history class. I was having the multimonitor maze dream again. It's a recurring dream I have when I feel worried. I know this for a fact because scientific evidence links dreams with emotions, and dreaming about being lost is a big sign of anxiety. In the dream, I'm trying to find my way home, and I'm surrounded by a maze of computer monitors. A zillion of them. At first, it seems like a dream come true to have so many monitors in one place. But then all the monitors start buzzing with static. And no matter which way I turn in the maze, I can never find my way out.

I'm lost. Trapped in a buzzing multimonitor maze.

That night, just as I was about to go to sleep, I heard a *DING*. I thought it was my phone, but when I looked down, I saw the ding had come from my Moon Scanner. TARGET FOUND! flashed across the screen in red letters. I was on my own this time. Casey wasn't able to film us that night because she had to cram for an English test.

Me and Devil arrived at the location identified by the Moon Scanner. It was an abandoned subway tunnel. I was relieved because this was a familiar environment to me. I was used to moving around in tunnels. A worker from the power company was connecting an electrical wire to underground lines. I watched him wipe sweat from his forehead, and then he climbed up out of the tunnel through a manhole.

As soon as he was out of my sight, I whispered to Devil, "C'mon!"

I made my way down the dark, dusty tunnel with Devil right behind me. I swept my Moon Scanner back and forth. Up ahead, the tunnel curved. Light flashed from beyond the bend. We slowly moved forward.

We ended up in a huge room with six generators thrumming. Lightning flashed and crackled in the room. I peeked around one of the generators. *Aftershock!* But she wasn't in her fully charged-up mode. I could see her real face and blond hair. She was slumped over with her eyes closed, holding on to two of the generators as electricity coursed into her body. She was feeding and restoring her energy. I stayed hidden and double-checked my Bubble Blaster. After several minutes, she slowly began rising in the air, glowing brighter and brighter.

I jumped out and fired. *BLOOOP!* The bubble completely enveloped Aftershock. She opened her eyes and looked stunned. The bubble rolled backward.

I called out to Devil, "Now, D!"

"*ROOOAR!*" Devil charged the bubble and kicked it, sending it bouncing around like a beach ball.

"That's right, Electrical Lady!" I said. "It's time for you to bounce outta the LES."

"*ROOOOAR, ROOOAR!*" Devil used his feet and tail to bat the bubble around. The bubble bounced behind an equipment rack. Devil tried to get to it, but he couldn't reach.

Then *BOOM!* Aftershock blasted the bubble apart with a burst of lightning. She rose into the air, grinning and glowing blue.

"Sorry to burst your bubble," Aftershock said. She snapped her fingers, and the whole room went dark. Totally black. *KRAKOOM!* Lightning struck right between me and Devil, sending us both flying through the air.

Devil howled. I had never heard him make that sound before, and it pierced right through my heart. Another lightning bolt just missed me, and I ran for cover. Aftershock laughed. I clicked my goggles to activate night vision. As soon as I could see Aftershock, I skated as fast as I could toward her, launching myself into the air with my boxing gloves ready.

SNAG! Aftershock grabbed me right out of the air. I could see Devil's tail flailing as he lashed out blindly at Aftershock. He howled and howled. I wanted to get to him so I could calm him down. Then *CRACK!* Lightning knocked me over, and I tumbled farther away from Devil. I fell against a generator and must have hit my head, because I felt woozy. I grabbed my head, and the whole room was spinning.

Then suddenly my night vision went blank. Complete darkness again. Aftershock had yanked my helmet and goggles off. She stood over me with her glowing, sparking fists raised and ready to strike. Then she hesitated.

"Holy puberty!" Aftershock said. "You're just a kid?"

"A-doy. My name is Moon Girl. It's right in the name, lady."

I saw Devil creeping up behind Aftershock.

"I could never hurt a child," Aftershock said. Then she shrugged. "But I should at least try."

Aftershock was about to pound me with her fists. Then Devil charged at her. But she heard him coming and spun around. Aftershock blasted Devil with multiple lightning bolts.

"Devil!" I shouted. He fell backward and moaned in pain.

Aftershock's powerful blasts ricocheted off the walls and hit the generators. I heard a sizzling sound and smelled burning. The room was on fire. Aftershock flew above the fire, up in the air, and out a door at the top of a metal staircase. I picked up my helmet and goggles and staggered over to Devil Dinosaur.

"Devil! Say something!" I shrieked. "C'mon,

get up. We gotta go. We gotta get out of here."
The fire was spreading, and smoke filled
the air.

Devil whimpered and moaned. I shook
him gently.

But he wasn't moving.

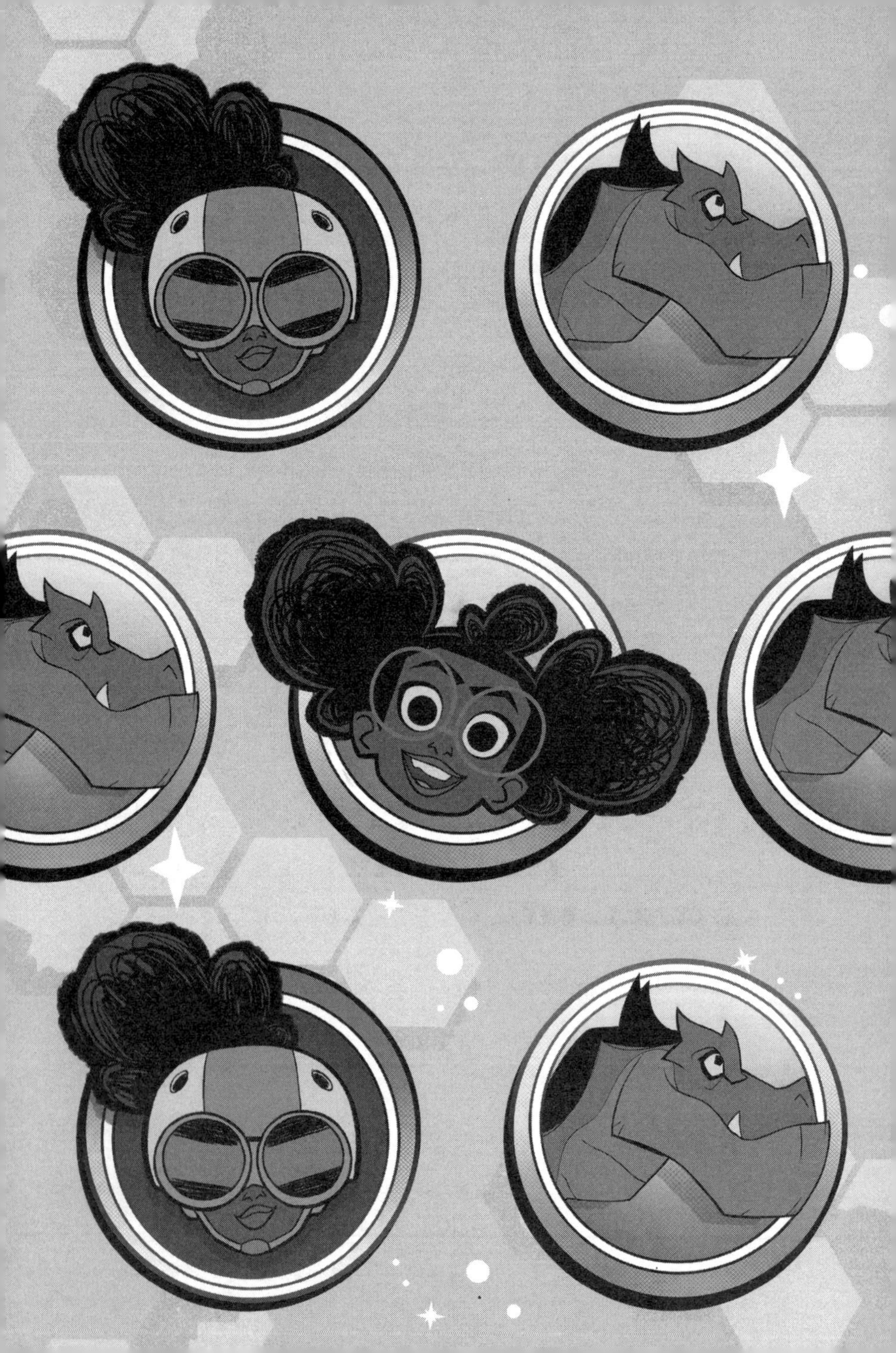

CHAPTER ELEVEN

Time was running out, and I was having a total meltdown. It was a good thing Aftershock didn't see me like that. I was crying and shaking and gasping for air.

I was scared, but I was also furious. I thought about what Iron Man would do. He wouldn't stand there bawling his eyes out. He would power up his suit. And after attacking anything in his way, he would pick up Devil, fly through the air, and carry him all the way home. I couldn't do any of those things. But I knew Devil and I had a strong connection. If anyone could get him up, it was me.

I stroked his head and leaned in close to him.

"Devil, this place is on fire, and I need you!" I said. "Please get up! I'm not leaving you here. I'm gonna help you get better. And when you get better, we'll have monster movie night, and you'll get to eat popcorn and hot dogs. Lots of hot dogs. But we gotta get out of here first."

Devil groaned and slowly picked himself up. His tail and multiple spots on his body were scorched. He staggered around like he was disoriented. I guided him through the tunnel and patted him gently on the side.

"Let's go home," I said.

When I looked back, all I saw were orange flames blazing.

I slept in Devil's den that night. I knew if I slept in my bedroom, I would keep getting up all night to check on him. I still stayed up all night checking on him, but I was right by his side. Sometimes he snored. Other times he whimpered. As long as he was making noise, at least I knew he was still breathing.

The next morning, Devil groaned while I slathered ointment on his wounds. His tongue rolled out of his mouth as he tried to reach the ointment.

"Don't lick it," I said. I put the lid back on the jar and forced a smile. I held back tears because I didn't want Devil to see me crying.

"Now get some rest," I said. "You'll be okay."

As soon as I turned away, my eyes filled with tears. Casey came over to help. When I saw her, I immediately burst into tears. I couldn't hold it in.

"Oh, no!" Casey said, giving me a big hug.

"What are we gonna do, Casey? Devil's hurt bad. Are we in over our heads?"

"No . . . I don't know," she said. "We'll figure

it out together." She gave me tissues and a mirror, and I cleaned up my face.

The home monitor crackled, and we heard Mom's voice.

She said, "Lunella isn't up yet? It's almost time for school."

I needed to get up to the apartment fast. Casey checked her phone.

"Yikes!" Casey said. "We gotta go."

I darted back up the steps and kissed Devil on the snout.

"Heal up," I said. "I'll check on you later."

Devil grunted and smiled at me as he drifted off to sleep.

Me and Casey made our way back to my room. Then we slowly tiptoed through the apartment hallway. I helped Casey slip out the front door without anyone noticing. Then I peeked into the kitchen. My dad was leaning over the stove scrambling eggs. Mom, Mimi, and Pops were sitting at the kitchen table drinking coffee.

"Now, not too runny with those eggs, James," Mimi said.

"I know, Ma," Dad said, flipping them with his spatula.

Pops clicked on the kitchen television and turned it to the news.

The TV news announcer said, "Yet another blackout overnight, and police finally have a suspect. Power company employees spotted Moon Girl and Devil Dinosaur fleeing the scene. Citizens are asked to report any sightings of the duo, described as a teen girl on skates and, uh, a big red lizard."

Uh-oh! This was an unexpected development. I had never imagined that I would become a suspect. "Not Moon Girl!" Mom said. "She did so much good for folks around here! I don't buy it. She can't be behind the blackouts."

Pops said, "Told you it was that no-good dino! Bet he dragged Moon Girl into it. His name ain't Angel Dinosaur."

"I just wonder where the parents are," Dad said. "They gotta be all kinds of dumb to not know what their own kid is up to."

"Let's not rush to judgment," Mimi said. "We may not have the full story yet."

I walked through the kitchen fast and grabbed a piece of toast.

"Hi, Mom. Hi, Dad. Hi, Pops. Hi, Mimi. Sorry, I'm late for school!" I sped from the kitchen and ran out the front door.

Mom called after me, "Lunella!" But I kept going. I had to get out of there.

All the way to school, I thought about what the news announcer had said. *Police finally have a suspect. Employees spotted Moon Girl and Devil Dinosaur fleeing the scene.*

Later that day in science class, I watched the clock, which seemed like it wasn't budging. The day dragged on and on. I drew pictures of Devil Dinosaur with little red hearts in my notebook while Coach Hbrek stumbled through the science lesson.

"So, ah, protons and electrons are like, uh, I guess like offense and defense. If you lose an electron, it's like a red card in soccer. It puts you down a player."

Then I heard a familiar voice, which made me look up from my Devil Dinosaur doodles.

"Your analogy was pretty rad, Coach," a lady said. All the kids turned to look at the blond woman in the classroom doorway. When I saw her, I almost fell out of my chair. I recognized her right away. Aftershock in street clothes! She extended her hand to Coach Hbrek.

"I'm Ms. Allison Dillon," she said. "I'm the new science teacher. Hooray! You're saved!"

Coach looked relieved and handed her his marker for the whiteboard.

"Great! I was running out of sports analogies," Coach said. "And, hey, if you ever get stuck, just ask our resident genius—Lunella Lafayette. She's as smart as they come!" Coach pointed at me. Ms. Dillon stared at me. I could see from her face that she recognized me. Her initial shock turned into a sinister smirk.

"Oh, I'm sure she is," Ms. Dillon said.

The bell rang. We all jumped up. Kids started filing out of the room.

Ms. Dillon said, "Could you stay after class a minute, Lunella Lafayette?"

I froze. Now she knew my name. What did she want from me?

"Ooooooh," Eduardo said. "You're already in trouble."

"Get out of here, Eduardo," I said. He flipped a loser hand sign at me and ran out of the room.

Ms. Dillon shut the door.

"What are you doing here?" I asked.

Ms. Dillon said, "What? Me? Why? The Lower East Side is my home now. *Su casa, mi casa!*"

"But you're stealing all our power! And 'cause no one gives a rip about us, you think we're easy pickings!"

"To quote you, a-doy. And being a disarmingly attractive science teacher is the perfect cover. And there's a handy charging spot right around the corner, so I can hit it before dinner."

Eduardo barged back in. He was driving me crazy. I spun around to face him.

"Read the room, Eduardo! Get out!" I shouted.

"I forgot my basketball," he said. "Jeez, so touchy. . . . You must really be in big trouble." He grabbed his ball and left. As soon as he shut the door, I turned back to Ms. Dillon.

"Listen up, Geek Lightning," I said. "I'm not gonna let you bleed the Lower East Side dry. Devil and I are gonna—"

"Let me stop you right there, Fun Size," Ms. Dillon said. "First of all, Geek Lightning was surprisingly hurtful. Second, if I don't get my daily jolt, I lose my power, my mojo. Ya feel me? And that ain't happening. You want an A in my class? Then hang up your cape and stop annoying me. You're not a real Super Hero."

"Well, you're not a real blonde," I said. I was proud of myself because a lot of times I have to think up clever things to say in advance. Like Geek Lightning, for example. Back in the lab, I had made an entire list of other names I could call Aftershock. But I thought of saying she wasn't a real blonde right off the top of my head. It was the truth, too. I could see her dark roots.

"Okay, that just got you an F for today," she said. "Happy? Now do the math on this." She had an evil look in her eyes. Then she tapped the light switch and transformed into Aftershock. Then *whomp!* The school went dark. Aftershock had caused another blackout.

I could hear chaos in the hallway. People were shouting and scrambling around. Then Aftershock glowed and levitated forward. I flinched and stumbled backward.

"I'm far more powerful than you'll ever be," she said. "So step off . . . or I'll do to your family what I did to your dinosaur."

Hold up—now Aftershock was threatening my family?

See, this is exactly why Super Heroes are supposed to keep their identities secret.

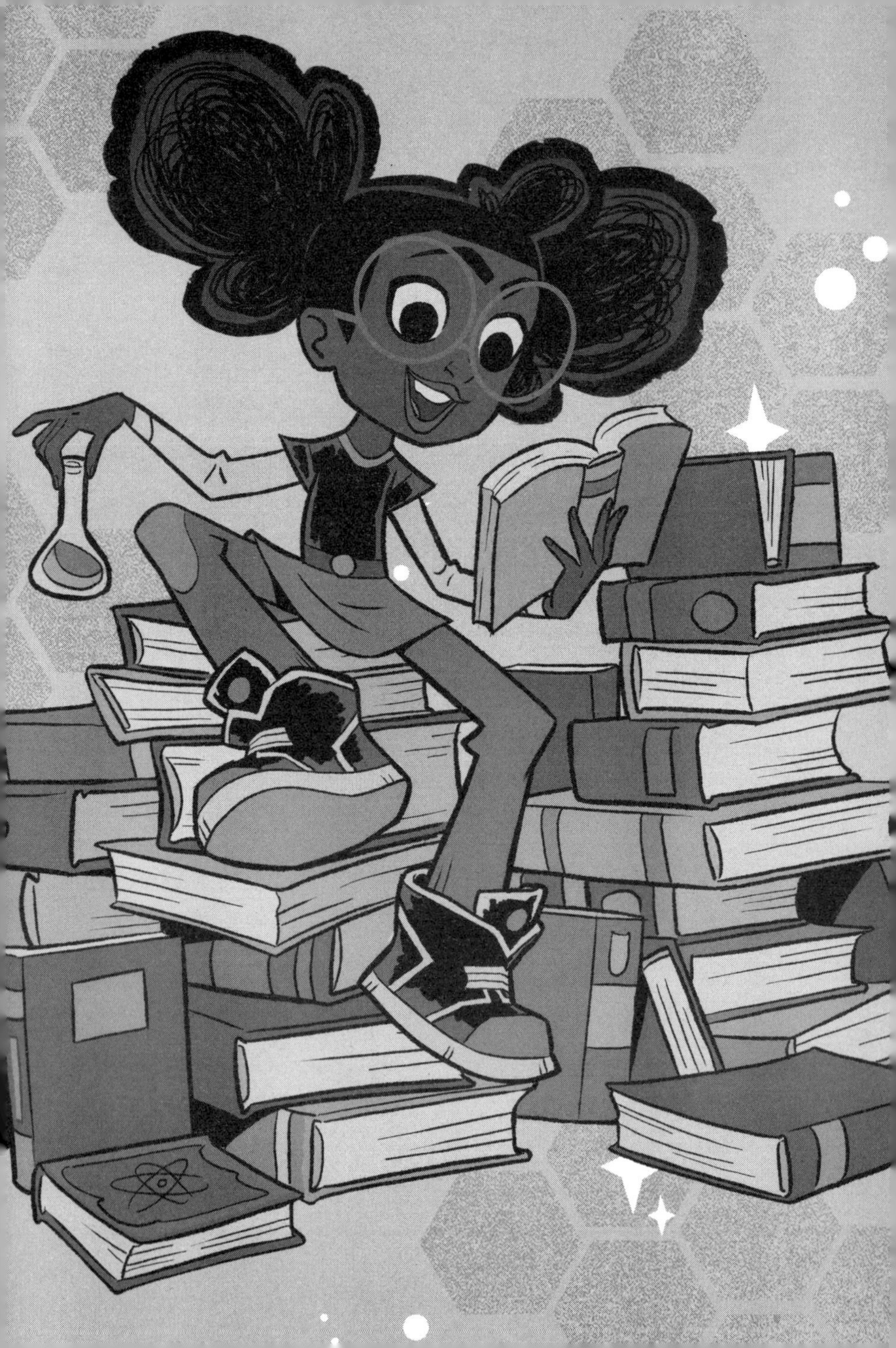

CHAPTER TWELVE

The power was back, and so was Ms. Dillon. All traces of Aftershock were gone by the time I left the science classroom.

Ms. Dillon smiled and pretended we had been chatting about homework. What a fake!

"And be sure to read chapter five by tomorrow, m'kay?" Ms. Dillon said.

"Hey, did you guys see the blackout?" Eduardo asked as everyone in the school hallway headed to their next class. "Bet that Moon Girl did it!"

I couldn't even speak to them anymore. The combination of Aftershock's threat and Eduardo's accusation made me so mad. If I didn't get out of there, I was going to explode like a volcano. I was sure lava was about to erupt from my ears.

I grabbed my backpack and pushed past Eduardo. As soon as I left the room, I sent Casey an emergency text message: *NEED to talk. Meet me after school. Big news about Aftershock!*

On my way home, I kept replaying my conversation with Aftershock—rolling it over in my mind. By the time Casey arrived, I had written everything down so I could tell her exactly what happened. She listened carefully.

"What?" Casey shrieked after I finished.

"Yeah, Aftershock, aka the Electrical Lady, aka Ms. Dillon, is my *science teacher* now."

Casey paced back and forth. She raised her eyebrows and tilted her head to the side, and I could see her wheels turning. She was thinking up a new plan. But I didn't want a new plan. I wanted out.

"So glad I'm not in fifth period science," Casey said. "Okay, new plan: You build a gadget to blast her butt. I'll get the keys to the teachers' lounge, then we hide there till she—"

I interrupted her. "No. It's over, Casey."

"Huh? What do you mean 'over'?" She walked toward me and looked serious.

"I mean it's over," I said. "No more Super-Heroing. First I put Devil in danger, and now my family is in danger, too. I already feel horrible because Devil got hurt. If Aftershock hurt my parents or Pops or Mimi, I would never forgive myself."

"But you and Devil were just finding your groove! You can handle this lady."

"But look at him!" I said. Casey followed me up to Devil's den. Devil snorted in his sleep. He tossed and turned like he couldn't get comfortable. I stroked his tail softly. That always seemed to calm him down.

"He didn't ask for any of this," I whispered. "It's my fault he's even here. So I have to send him back. It's what's best for him. He'll be safer this way."

"*Send him back?* You don't know that. We can figure this out. There's gotta be a way."

"No, Casey. Aftershock is just too powerful. And now she's got me boxed in a corner. I can't fix this."

"But what happened to 'One girl can make a difference'? And what about Moon Girl magic? Huh? Was all that just *basura*?"

I picked up my Moon Girl costume and held it in the air. I loved the moon Casey had put on my helmet. It was hard letting go of Moon Girl, but I felt like I didn't have a choice.

"I was wrong, okay? I got in way over my head, and I just can't do it anymore."

Casey started, "But—"

"I said I can't!" I shouted. "Now stop pushing me!" I threw my costume at Casey, and she caught it.

"If that's the way you feel, then I guess you don't need me, either," Casey said as she walked to the elevator. She turned back for a second and looked at me.

"I understand you don't want anything bad to happen to your family. But I believed in you, you know," she said.

As I watched Casey leave, I felt awful. I went up to Devil's den to check on him. He opened his eyes, and I rubbed his snout.

"You doin' okay, buddy?"

He grunted, telling me he was fine.

"Hey, now that you're feeling better, let's put on some flicks. We can hang out. Just you and me. Big day tomorrow." I didn't tell him what I meant by that. The big day was that I was going to be sending him back through the portal. I decided to break the news to him in the morning.

We watched two monster movies while I cuddled up in Devil's tail. We munched on popcorn, and I knew he was starting to feel like his old self, because he ate a bunch of hot dogs.

And he grunted like he was happy. After we ate, I brushed Devil's teeth and sprayed his mouth with a concoction I made in the lab. He liked the peppermint taste. We snuggled up for a long time, even after the movies ended, and it was a lot easier to snuggle with a dinosaur who smelled like peppermint instead of hot dogs.

When we woke up the next morning, I wondered if I could go through with it. Bringing a *T. rex* to New York City was the best thing that had ever happened to me. Could I really send Devil away? But I also knew that I didn't want him to be hurt or worse. I didn't want anyone getting hurt. I just couldn't risk it.

I activated the portal generator. When I checked the gauge, I confirmed what I already knew: there was only enough juice for a one-way trip. Devil woke up when he heard the noise. He lumbered down from his den.

"Mroo?" he said. He wanted to know what was going on.

"Look, the thing is . . . New York stinks,

right? It's no place for a dinosaur. You oughta go home where you'll be safe. Okay?" The portal was open, but Devil didn't budge. He just snorted and stared at me. I grabbed a handful of hot dogs from the mini fridge.

"Hey—hey, look! You hungry? Breakfast time!" I tossed the hot dogs through the portal.

"Go get 'em, Devil!" Devil sniffed after the hot dogs. But he still didn't budge. I got behind him and tried to push him. No movement.

I was getting desperate. The portal would be open for only a small window of time.

"Fine! You want the truth?" I yelled at Devil. "I don't want you anymore. You're nothing but a pain in my butt. So time to go—go! Get out!" Tears started streaming down my face.

"Just go, you big dumb lizard!"

Devil's eyes looked so sad. He took a step toward the portal, then another. He looked back at me. I wiped away the tears and tried to look tough. He finally turned away . . . and headed through the portal.

I left the lab and didn't look back. I threw myself on my bed and cried into a pillow for an hour. I told myself at least crying has positive biological effects. Emotional tears help the body get rid of stress hormones and toxins.

Then I convinced myself that without Moon Girl and Devil Dinosaur, I could get back to being by myself most of the time. And I would have more time in my lab for projects and experiments I had started and never finished. But the problem with this plan was that deep down I didn't want to be by myself. And I didn't want to be in my lab, either, because it reminded me of Devil and Casey.

So I stayed out of my lab. In the school cafeteria, I picked at my food at lunchtime. Eduardo and Anand tried to get me to do the puzzle cube trick, but I wasn't in the mood. Every time they bugged me, I pushed the cube away. I caught a glimpse of Casey that afternoon. She looked at me for a couple of seconds and walked away.

My neighborhood was a mess. More businesses closed. The pawn shop was busy, but Mr. Septimus told me that was because more people needed to sell their belongings to make money. Blackouts and burglaries were still happening, and Ahmed's windows got smashed. Big spools of wire were abandoned on the sidewalk. The power company had left them behind as if they had given up on helping the LES. This was not the LES I knew. I couldn't even look the shop owners in the eye anymore, because I had let them down.

And just when I thought things couldn't get worse, I showed up at the roller rink after school and saw my parents nailing up a sign with big red letters:

FOR SALE.

Everything that was happening made me feel like I would never skate, dance, or sing along to music ever again. I just couldn't imagine wanting to do those things. And that was an awful feeling.

CHAPTER THIRTEEN

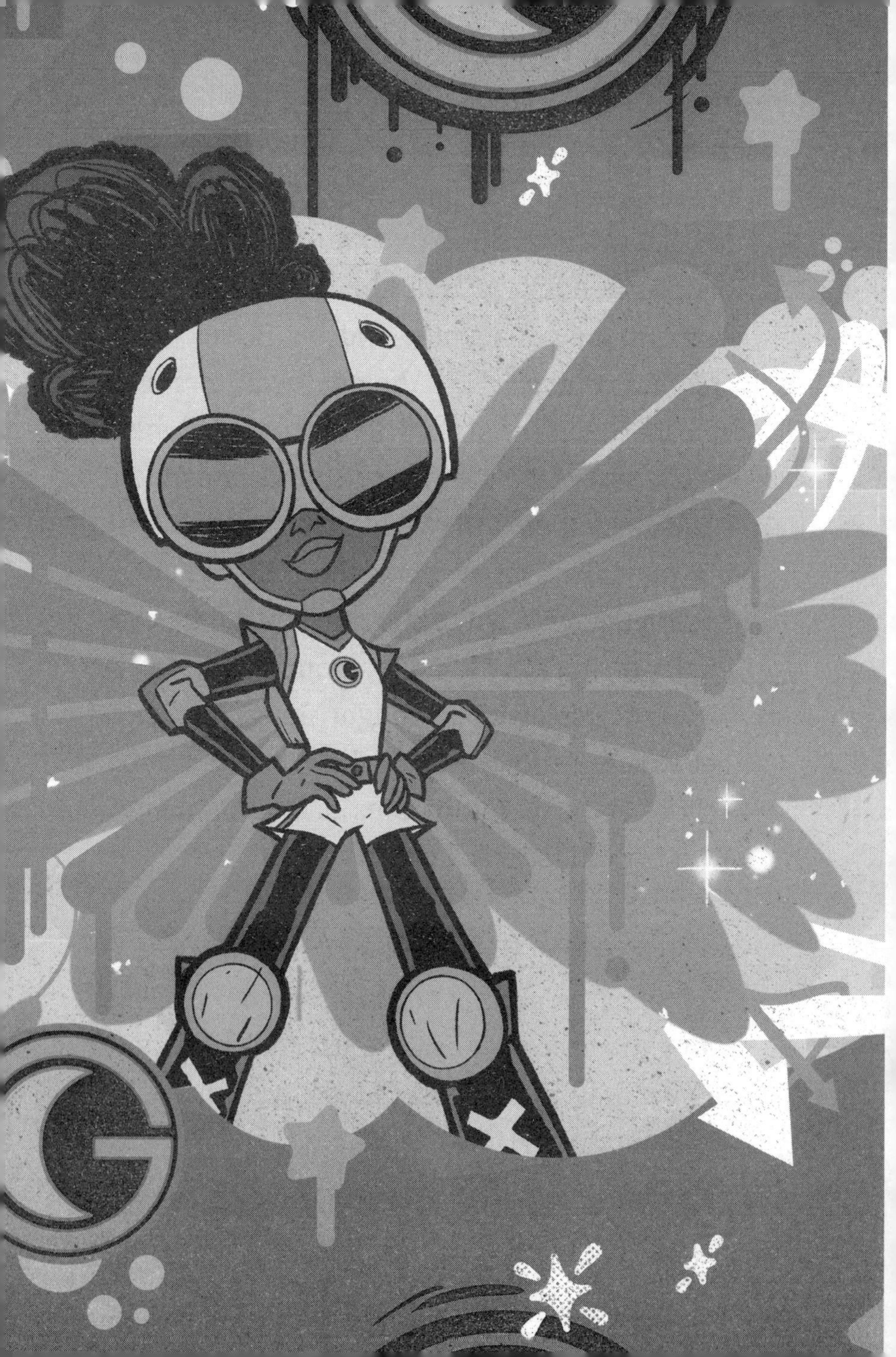

I ran home as fast as I could and didn't look back. Roll With It was Pops's big dream, and the rink meant everything to our family. I couldn't imagine life without it.

When I got to our apartment, I rushed through the door in tears. I had planned on crawling under the covers and staying in bed for the rest of the year. But Mimi stopped me in the living room.

"Whoa, whoa, whoa, slow down, child," Mimi said. "What's wrong?"

I paused for a moment. I had to say something, because Mimi wasn't going to just let me slip away in silence.

"I saw the 'for sale' sign," I told her. "I know we're selling the rink, and it's all because of me."

"Hold on. How do you figure that it's all because of you?"

I wondered how much I should tell her. Mimi has a warm, soothing way about her that makes me want to spill everything. So I had to be careful.

"Cause I'm . . . well, I fix things," I told her. "That's what I'm good at. And I wanted to fix this blackout problem for the LES. And if I'm supposed to be so smart, why couldn't I figure it out?"

"Come here," Mimi said. She took my hands and pulled me over to the couch.

"This is not on you," Mimi said as we sat

down. "Even the smartest girl in the world can't do everything. That's why you gotta lean on the people who love you. And those are some solid people. You got me and Pops, your mom and dad—and that new friend of yours, right?"

"Yeah, Casey," I said. "But I kinda messed that up, too."

"Well, if you're looking to fix something, it's never too late," Mimi said. "If you really want it, you can get a second chance." Mimi always knows what she's talking about. Hearing it from her made a second chance sound possible. I wasn't sure what I would say to Casey, but maybe I could go see her and at least apologize for throwing my costume at her.

"You're right. Thanks, Mimi," I said. "I'll go see Casey."

I swung the front door open to leave, and Casey was standing there. She was just about to push the buzzer.

"Oh! Hi," I said.

"Hi," Casey said.

"I was . . . This is kinda weird. I was just coming to see you."

"Yeah, I was coming to see if . . ." We both laughed.

"C'mon in," I said.

Mimi winked at us. "I'll make you girls some brownies." Mimi really is the best grandma on the planet.

Casey followed me to my bedroom. I closed the door and turned toward her.

"Look, I . . . I'm sorry, Casey. I know I'm goin' through some stuff, but I shouldn't have taken it out on you. I shouldn't have thrown my costume at you. I shouldn't have pushed you and Devil away."

"No, me too. I get where you are coming from. You should know that with or without Moon Girl, I'm still your BFF, Lunella. And don't worry. I took down the website, tossed the costume, all that junk. Guess I can be a bit much. That's what the other kids say."

"Well, I think you're exactly the right amount," I said.

"You know, you're pretty much the first real friend I ever had, Lu."

"You too, Case," I said. Casey's face lit up.

"Look at us! Do we use nicknames now?"

"I guess we do!" We hugged for a long time. Then I stepped back with my hands still on Casey's shoulders.

"Listen, I don't know if I have a chance against Aftershock. And I don't know what will happen if I fail. But I know what'll happen if I don't even try. I need to be Moon Girl again."

"Lu, are you sure?" Casey asked.

"There's no one else to stick up for the Lower East Side. Just me."

"Okay, then I'm really glad to hear that, because . . ." Casey grinned and pulled the Moon Girl costume from her bag.

"I never shut the site down! Ta-da! Here's your costume. Let's do this. Woo-hoooooo!"

"OMG, yes!" I said. "Moon Girl magic!"

Then I told Casey how I'd sent Devil back through the portal.

"I made a horrible mistake," I said. "I really miss him!"

We stayed in my bedroom and had a brainstorming/pep talk/planning session while demolishing a whole plate of brownies.

First we made a checklist of all the things that empowered me. Because when times got tough, I needed to be able to look at that list and remember everything on it instead of just falling apart. The original Moon Girl was at the top of the list, followed by research, roller-skating, and music. All the mixtapes my mom made me could get me into battle mode as Moon Girl.

Next we made another list of everything we had accomplished in such a short time.

"You created an entire five-year plan for us," I said. "With spreadsheets and Power-Point slides."

"And you created a device that brought a

dinosaur to New York City!" Casey said. "And you figured out how to communicate with him! You're a genius."

"Yup, I did do all that stuff," I said through a mouthful of brownies.

Finally, we made a list of all kinds of facts I had learned as part of my research on how to defeat Aftershock. I had studied everything there was to know about electrical energy.

Me and Casey mapped out a detailed plan to expose Aftershock as the real villain. And I remembered that I liked having someone who was in this with me.

The next afternoon, it was time to put our plan into motion.

With full Moon Girl costume and all my gear, I skated down the street at four p.m., weaving between cars. I wanted to attract attention, and it worked.

People on the street gasped and pointed at me.

"Hey, it's Moon Girl!" a man yelled.

A lady said, "Look, it's that Moon Girl character, the one causing all the blackouts."

Just as we'd thought, everyone still believed I was the baddie.

I hopped on the sidewalk. It felt incredible to be back in my skates, hearing the sound of my wheels rolling fast across the pavement. I didn't knock anybody over, but I bumped into a few elbows.

"Hey, watch it!" someone said. "What is she doing?"

"You wanna stop me?" I shouted. "You gotta catch me. C'mon, people!"

I looked back and saw people chasing me. The plan was working! *BEEP, BEEP, BEEP!* I glanced down at my Moon Scanner, which was tracking a signal.

The crowd following me grew bigger and bigger. The Moon Scanner kept beeping like crazy, so I knew I was on the right track. I caught a glimpse of Coach Hbrek and Eduardo in the crowd.

"What's goin' on?" Eduardo said. "It's Moon Girl!"

"That's right!" I said. "It's Moon Girl!"

The crowd followed me around the corner to a row of e-bike chargers. Ms. Dillon was connected to the chargers, glowing blue as energy coursed through her body. People pointed and screamed, stunned to see Ms. Dillon sparking with electricity. Casey ran up on the sidewalk, shooting video with her phone.

Then *whooomp!* Lights in nearby buildings went out. Another blackout. I pointed to Ms. Dillon.

"See?" I shouted. "Ms. Dillon is the real cause of the blackouts."

"Rad!" Eduardo said. "Ms. Dillon is a super villain!"

Coach Hbrek said, "Aw, man, now I gotta teach science again."

Ms. Dillon was furious—so mad that she fully transformed into Aftershock! Some people in the crowd stepped back. A bunch of people took out their phones to take pictures and shoot video.

Jimmy from Jimmy's Gym flexed his muscles and stepped forward, followed by Coach Hbrek and others in the crowd.

"All right, Electrical Lady," Jimmy said. "Let's dance!"

Aftershock said, "How 'bout the Electric Slide?"

FWOOM! Aftershock unleashed an electromagnetic burst, blasting Jimmy, Coach Hbrek, and the whole crowd backward.

"Hey!" I shouted. "You come for them, you're coming for me!"

Aftershock said, "Um, okay then—I'm comin' for you!"

I probably should have been scared. But I wasn't. I was ready to take Aftershock down and save the LES once and for all.

But first I turned my battle music all the way up!

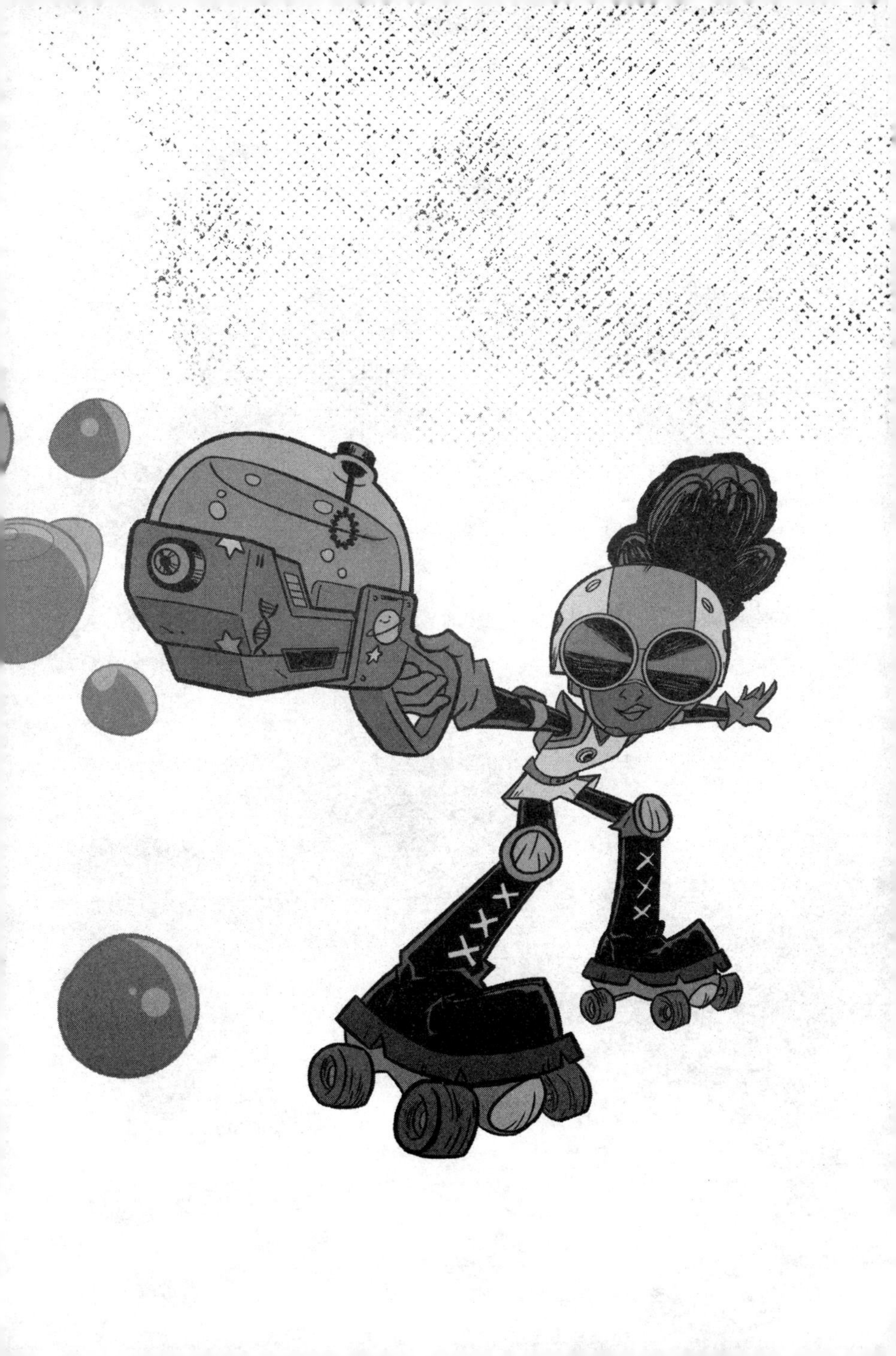

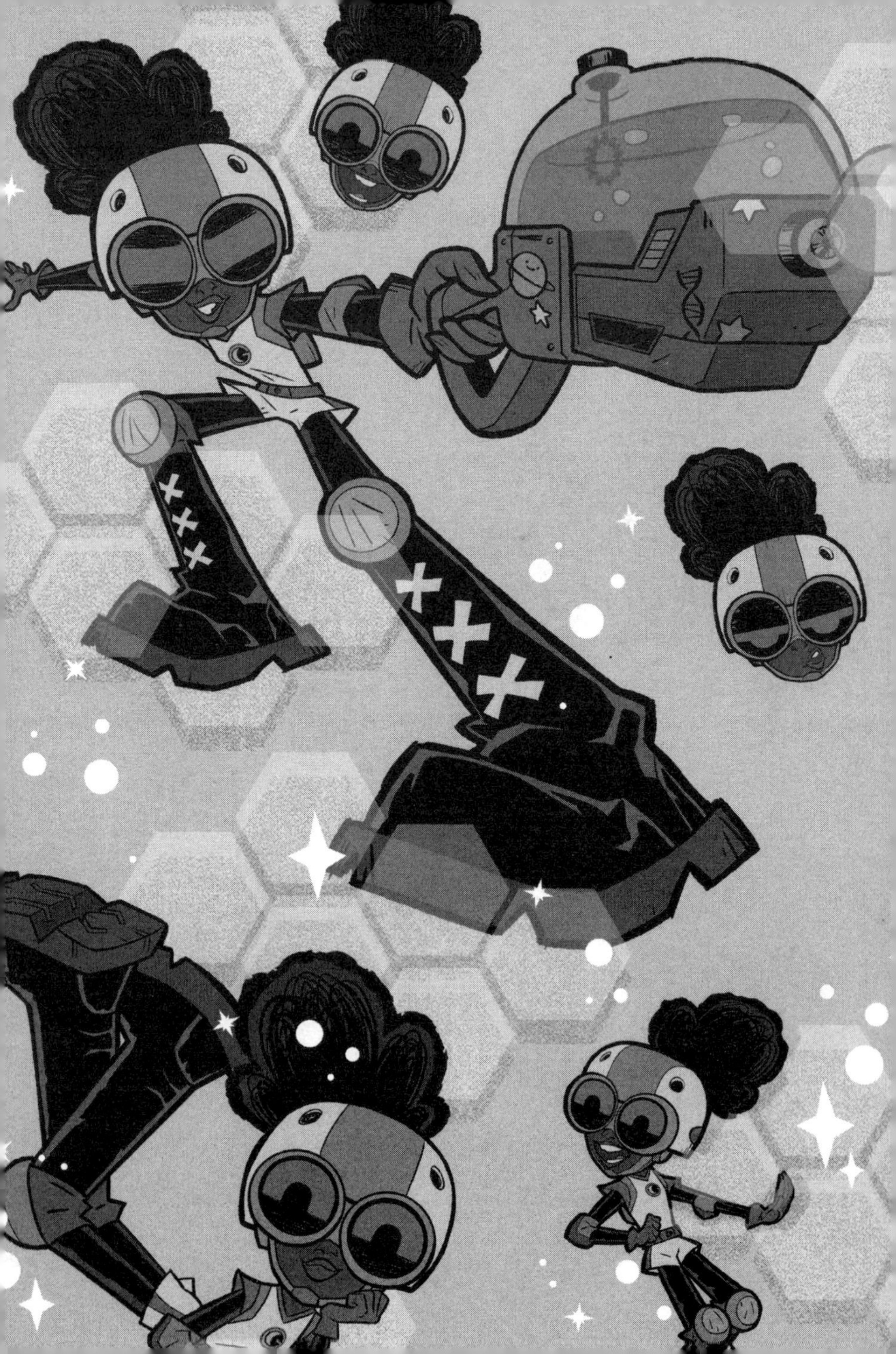

CHAPTER FOURTEEN

· · · · · · · · · · · · · · · · ·

Whether it's the super-fast beat of hip-hop or the smooth melody of rhythm and blues, music always lifts me up and makes me feel like anything is possible. With one of my favorite tunes blasting, I focused on dodging Aftershock's lightning bolts.

I skated in a zigzag motion across the park while pressing a newly installed button on my Moon Scanner. *BEEP, BEEP, BEEP!* The Moon

Scanner was activated for the next phase of my plan. I headed for the center of the park, with Aftershock hot on my trail. As she levitated through the air, electricity crackled and sparked all around her.

C'mon, I thought. *Keep following me!* I wanted to lure her to just the right spot. In the center of the park, there was a dry fountain. I raced around to the other side of the fountain. Then I turned and watched Aftershock getting closer and closer. *C'mon!* She was almost right where I needed her to be.

"Wait for it. Wait for it," I said.

As soon as Aftershock hovered over the right spot, I raised my Moon Scanner in the air.

"Yes!" I shouted, clicking the button. "Electricity and H_2O don't mix, sister!"

But nothing happened.

"Nuh-uh!" I said. "What?"

Well, here's what was supposed to happen: The fountain was supposed to turn on.

Water was supposed to shoot out from the ground and douse Aftershock. The impurities in the water were supposed to conduct electricity and electrocute her with a high voltage of energy.

I clicked the button again, harder. Still nothing.

Aftershock laughed and moved away from the fountain. The fountain finally turned on, but it was too late. *SPLOOSH! SPLOOSH!* Water shot up behind Aftershock, missing her by just a few feet.

"Dang Internet lag!" I said. I had hacked into the city's park system to turn on the fountain with my Moon Scanner. But a bad connection messed up the timing.

I looked up from the Moon Scanner, and Aftershock was aiming right for me. I thought that was the end of me. I didn't have time to skate away and dodge her this time.

Aftershock yelled, "Sayonara, sister!"

Then *BOOM, BOOM, BOOM!* Something

huge ran up behind Aftershock. I couldn't make out what it was because the creature was hidden behind the fountain spray. Then *SPLOOSH!* The humongous shadowy figure slammed into Aftershock, hurling her over me through the air. She crashed through the window of a nearby building. *CRASH, BOOM!*

Aftershock screamed, *"AAAAAGH!"*

As the water from the fountain slowed down, I spotted a tail. I recognized that creature.

Devil!

I skated over to him, and he bent his head down and nudged me. I reached up and touched his snout.

"You're here? You stayed? How? But that was your only chance to get home!"

Devil replied in grunts and snorts. Turned out he had come back through the portal before it closed, and he'd been in my lab waiting for me.

For a minute, we all forgot the fact that Aftershock had just crashed through a window. The LES crowd came closer to me and Devil. They listened to us talking.

"What did he say?" Eduardo shouted.

"Yeah, what's he talking about?" someone else yelled.

I turned to the crowd.

"He said the Lower East Side is his home now, and that his home is worth fighting for. And he said I'm worth fighting for." I hugged Devil's head.

"I love you, Devil Dinosaur!" I told him. Then I shouted to everyone, "Aftershock hurt my dinosaur, ya know. And nobody messes with my dinosaur!" Everybody cheered. Devil purred and grinned.

A bunch of people in the crowd said, "Awww!"

I saw Casey nearby, wiping away tears as she filmed it all.

"This is my best work ever," Casey said. "Okay, everyone, that's a wrap."

Then *SMASH!* Aftershock busted out of

the building. She was in a rage, glowing blue and sparking with electricity.

She began firing lightning bolts at us.

I shouted, "Run, Devil, run!"

Aftershock didn't let up. She kept firing, searing the ground every time she missed us. Then *VOOOM!* Aftershock flew after us, and people in the crowd ran and scattered. For a few moments, she disappeared, and we weren't sure where she was.

Casey ran up to me.

"Lu, what are you gonna do? She's like living lightning."

"She's like lightning, all right, and so on to plan B. We gotta ground her!"

"You mean send her to her room and take her phone?" Casey said.

"No, I mean electrical grounding. Here's what we're gonna do. We're gonna hit her with a metal lightning rod that's connected to a wire leading underground. If we do it right, all of her electricity will be absorbed and dissipated safely. Oh, how I love science! We just need a big enough lightning rod! Okay, D, listen up."

I whispered in Devil's ear. He grunted and grinned.

"Ready? Let's go!" As Devil thundered off on his mission, I shouted after him, "You got this, D!"

Then I leapt into the air and popped out my brand-new gadget—Hoverwings! Wings with turbines on the tips.

"Aftershock isn't the only one who can fly," I said.

A new plan also meant I needed to switch my tunes again. I glanced down at the Moon Scanner and made the change.

Aftershock chased me as I flew through the LES. Now I just needed my new invention to keep working so I wouldn't crash to the ground. I hadn't had time to thoroughly test it.

"C'mon, Hoverwings," I said. "Don't fail me now!"

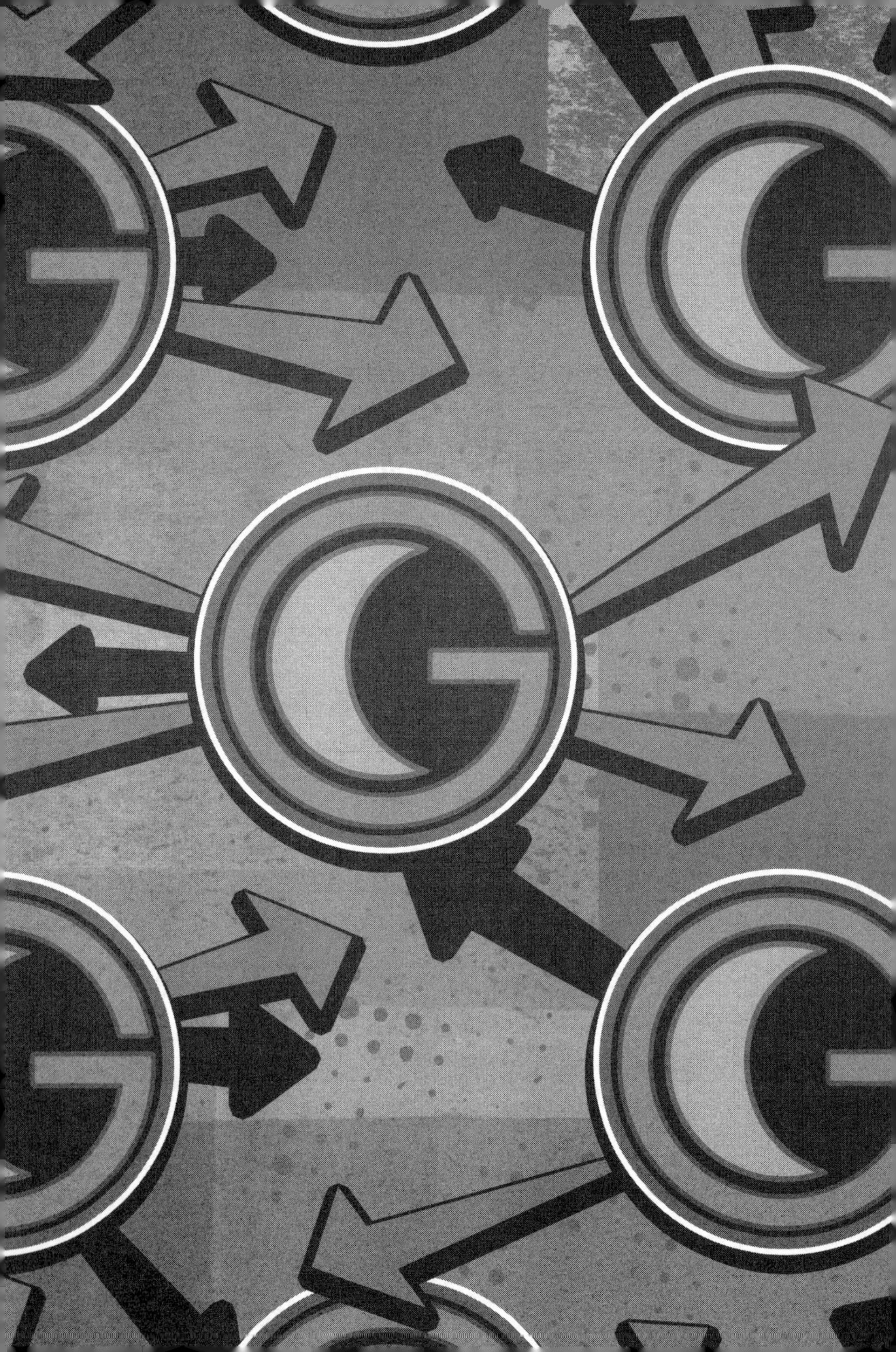

CHAPTER FIFTEEN

Soaring through the LES felt exhilarating! It was so amazing to fly above the crowd and over taxicabs. But the thing about flying fast was that it was hard for me to slow down and control my turns. I needed to keep Aftershock busy until Devil returned, so I led her on a chase. I had to pay attention to everything in front of me and keep track of where she was at the same time.

Just as I turned a corner, Aftershock

snuck up beside me. She startled me, which made me wobble to the side. I turned around awkwardly and ended up face to face with her. Much closer than I meant to be. So I slammed her with my boxing glove. Underneath each glove was another one, allowing me to jab her repeatedly.

"How many boxing gloves do you have?" Aftershock asked.

"It's gloves all the way down, baby!" I said, zooming away. Sirens wailed in the distance. Aftershock heard the sirens, too, and she pulled back.

I hovered in front of Roll With It. When I looked back, Aftershock was nowhere in sight.

"Lost her!" I said. "At least for now." I spotted one of the power company's huge spools of wire, with its end hanging down into a manhole. I flew toward it. Suddenly, my family walked around the corner. It was so weird seeing my parents, Pops, and Mimi—with me as Moon Girl flying above them. They looked up and down Delancey Street.

"What the heck is going on out here, Moon Girl?" Pops said.

"Hey! Uh, civilians! Take cover!" I said. Then *BAM!* A lightning bolt hit my Hover-wings, and I fell to the ground. One of my turbines sparked, grinding to a halt as Aftershock flew above us.

Aftershock flew toward me with her electric fists sparking. My mom darted over and stood between us. I didn't even know my mom could run that fast.

"*Nuh*-uh! Not today!" Mom said. Then the rest of my family circled me, along with others from the crowd.

Aftershock soared away as I picked myself up off the ground.

"Thank you," I said. I made my voice a little deeper, hoping they wouldn't recognize me.

"You all right, sweetheart?" Mimi asked.

"I'm okay," I said.

The truth was I felt like I might throw up any second, and my legs ached. But I mustered all my strength and skated down the street, unrolling the spool of wire along the way. That's when I saw Devil down the block. He was carrying a fifty-foot flagpole in his mouth.

"He did it!" I shouted. He had gotten the flagpole from outside of my school just like we planned. Devil charged toward me. When Aftershock started firing lightning bolts in his direction, Devil dodged them. He zigged and zagged and held on for as long as he could, but he dropped the flagpole, and it rolled into the street.

Meanwhile, my Hoverwings had stalled, so I stayed on the ground and concentrated on pushing the spool of wire. I realized the flagpole was too far away for me to reach it. Mimi was right when she said I can't do everything by myself.

I hollered, "Everybody, I need that flagpole!" The wire from the spool wasn't going to reach, and I needed to connect the wire to the flagpole.

Casey put her phone away. She ran to the pole and tried to lift it, but it was huge. Other people in the crowd approached Casey. LES shopkeepers, Coach Hbrek, and even the cops.

"Eduardo, *ayudame!*" Casey shouted.

Eduardo grabbed on to the flagpole, and everyone else followed. I watched as my family joined in, too. I wondered if they knew my secret. Did they know they were helping me? That I was Moon Girl?

Casey said, "Don't lift with your back! It's leg day, people! That means you, too, Jimmy!" Jimmy has the scrawniest legs ever. Still, he jumped in there to help. Everybody worked together to bring me the flagpole.

"Thank you!" I said. "Now move back and watch out, because I'm about to juice this up!" Everybody backed away as I slammed a panel shut on the turbine on my Hoverwings. I twisted the end of the wire around the flag-pole.

Devil ran toward me, with Aftershock flying right behind him. The pole was in the perfect position. Aftershock was going so fast, she couldn't stop. *KRA-THOOOM!* She slammed into the flagpole and gasped.

"We're taking our power back!" I said. Then *BOOM!* There was a mini explosion. On impact, Aftershock's full power coursed through the pole and crackled down the wire and into the ground. Through electrical grounding, we transferred electrons from Aftershock to the pole and then from the pole to the wire—sending Aftershock and her electrical charges literally into the earth. She vanished in a flash of energy.

Yes—victory! Aftershock was gone, and I was the one still standing. Devil licked me. "I've never been so happy to smell hot dog breath in my life!" I said. Even still, I planned to brush Devil's teeth and spray them down with peppermint mouthwash as soon as we got home.

As Aftershock's power dispersed across the Lower East Side, all the city lights came back on! And in that moment, I turned on victory music.

Below the gleaming Roll With It sign, everyone, including my family, surrounded me and Devil. Lower East Siders clapped and cheered and jumped up and down. And we all danced!

The next day, it was so cool to see that the spirit of the LES was back. Casey came up with an idea for me and Devil to make a special community appearance. I rode Devil down the street and waved as shop owners waved back at us.

Bubbe Bina waved and blew a kiss at me. The knish shop was back in business! Cops raised their coffee mugs. Señora Martinez tossed tamales to Devil, and he gobbled them up. At Roll With It, my family took down the FOR SALE sign.

And that's the story of how we saved the Lower East Side from the evil Aftershock and reclaimed our power.

My name is Lunella Lafayette, aka Moon Girl, and if you told me two months ago that one day I would be giving my dinosaur a bath at the car wash, helping my best friend at school plan her bat mitzvah, and inventing new devices to fight evil super villains, I never would have believed you. Not in a zillion years.